'Roxby's not the man you need.'

'What do you mean?' Alexandra fired back.

'I mean, if he was man enough to satisfy you in bed you wouldn't still be flashing fire and sending me sexual signals a man could read a mile off.'

'How dare you?' she breathed with concentrated fury.

'Believe me,' Jim answered abrasively, 'I dare plenty.'

She knew instinctively that to retaliate or to push him any further was simply asking for trouble. Normally, common sense would have stopped her. Now she seemed beyond the reach of caution.

'Try it and see where it gets you!' she said heatedly.

Suddenly there was so much static between them, she thought the air must snap with it. For a terrifying instant she was certain she'd gone too far. Jim's dark eyes glittered as they pierced hers. The racking moment dragged on, and then he said, menace in the lazy quietness of his voice, 'Let me tell you something as an old friend. Never issue a man with that kind of challenge unless you're prepared to take the consequences.'

THIS TIME, FOREVER

BY

JENNY ARDEN

MILLS & BOON LIMITED
ETON HOUSE   18-24 PARADISE ROAD
RICHMOND   SURREY   TW9 1SR

First published in Great Britain 1989 by Mills & Boon Limited

© Jenny Arden 1989

Australian copyright 1989 Philippine copyright 1989 This edition 1989

ISBN 0 263 76403 6

Set in English Times 10 on 11 pt. 01 – 8909 – 61628

Typeset in Great Britain by JCL Graphics, Bristol

Made and Printed in Great Britain

For Henry
Who opened my eyes to Italy
and to so many other places.

CHAPTER ONE

HIGH UP above the rough-cut coast, the rooftop terrace gave a sweeping view of the shimmering expanse of blue bay. The pink roofs of the pretty pastel and whitewashed houses showed among the lush green of the lemon groves, and a faint sultry breeze stirred like a warm caress. Light sparkled with dazzling brilliance off the invitingly blue water of the swimming pool, and over everything lay the somnolent afternoon heat.

Alexandra Challoner strolled towards one of the umbrella-topped tables. It was still fairly early in the season, and she had the terrace practically to herself. She threw her towel over the back of her deckchair and then stretched out lazily, letting her eyes rove to the limestone cliffs where the plants clambered for a foothold on the bare rock.

It would have been a waste to have cancelled the first week of their holiday in Sorrento just because her fiancé had been unable at the last minute to get away. Of course, she was missing him, but he had been right to insist that she go ahead without him, saying he'd join her as soon as he could.

She put her book down on the chair beside her and began to smooth some suntan cream on to her arms. As she did so, the sunlight made the solitaire diamond ring she wore on her engagement finger flash with rainbow brilliance. She looked at it and smiled. When she had been divorced three years ago, she had been so devastated that she had vowed she would never, *never* get entangled with a man again. Roxby had changed all

7

that, and the two of them were going to have a wonderful life together.

She reached her arms up and clasped her hands behind her head as she leaned back. Her blue eyes, with a hint of cobalt that radiated out from the pupils, were contented. The sun picked out burnished lights in her long fair hair that for once fell loose over her tanned shoulders. She was slim and supple with shapely legs, and her white bikini showed to advantage her graceful figure, the cleavage of her small breasts visible between the gold hoop that fastened her top at the front.

For the moment she wasn't in the mood to read. She closed her eyes, letting her thoughts drift. She couldn't get over her good fortune in falling in love with such a dependable and considerate man. With Roxby she felt so safe. She knew exactly the sort of life-style she had to look forward to when she became his wife. Theirs would be a real partnership, their careers dovetailing neatly, and with a host of other interests to cement their relationship.

In some ways it was a pity that her fiancé didn't want a family. At one time she had thought of having a baby with quite a wistful yearning, but instead she had concentrated on achieving her career ambitions which had been thwarted for so long. And, being realistic, with the way her marriage to Jim had turned out, it had all been for the best. Now, having suppressed her maternal instincts, she believed she was perfectly adjusted at almost thirty to the prospect of remaining childless and making her new marriage and her job her life.

She must have drifted off to sleep, for when she came back to reality more people had joined her on the terrace and the shadows were longer. Muted talk and laughter reached her from the nearby umbrella-shaded tables, while closer to the pool a showy brunette in the skimpiest of orange bikinis, a gold chain sparkling round her slim waist, was stretched out indolently on a sun-lounger.

Earlier, the mirrorlike surface of the pool had shimmered undisturbed. Now Alexandra could see the muscular back of a strong swimmer doing a lazily powerful crawl up the length of the pool. The animal grace of the man compelled her to watch him, and she noticed as the brunette pushed her sunglasses up on top of her head that she wasn't the only one whose interest had been caught by the swimmer.

He reached the end of the pool, turning underwater with such easy speed that the rhythm of his stroke didn't falter. Tanned shoulders rose powerfully again, the man's dark head lifting too briefly from the water for her to gain any impression of his features.

Yet suddenly a strange prickle of unease ran down Alexandra's spine. She sat up, disturbed by the raw male sexuality of the swimmer without knowing why. And then, as the man reached out a muscular arm to the tiled edge of the pool, shaking his head as he surfaced, she caught her breath with dismay.

Colour flamed and then died in her face as the man's dark eyes caught hers, his black, hawkish brows drawing together in a frown of recognition. This just wasn't possible! It simply couldn't be true that staying at the same hotel was her ex-husband, Jim Logan.

Her immediate instinct was to snatch up her towel and to sweep from the pool area with angry steps and her head held high. Instead, refusing to allow him to see how shaken she was, she steeled herself for a show of distant friendliness. After all, this wasn't the first time she'd seen Jim since they'd broken up, and the very purpose of an austerely civilised divorce was that when you met again afterwards it was with no bitter hostility—or at least, not on the surface.

Her mind flew back to the last time she'd seen her ex-husband, and she coloured again hotly. She would never work out how she could have so nearly let him seduce her. She pushed the memory away, giving him a cool smile, handling the shock staggeringly well, considering how she felt.

Jim hauled himself out of the pool with a litheness that was essentially and disturbingly male, while Alexandra forced herself to rally. She hadn't forgotten one single detail of his appearance, or the arrogant way he moved. Yet even so, as she saw the gleaming power of his broad shoulders and the tangle of dark hair on his chest, her heartbeat seemed to skip. His black trunks hugged his lean hips, and for an instant the thrusting aggressive quality of his masculinity made her feel almost panic-stricken.

'Alex—what a surprise!' he began, his tone holding a faintly abrasive note.

But, as though for formality's sake, he put a strong, tanned hand on her shoulder, bending to kiss her before he sat down in a deckchair beside her.

It was no more than a brush of the lips against her cheek, but she still flinched inwardly at the intimacy. After what had happened the last time, she didn't want him laying even the most casual hand on her, and she realised that it was going to take all her determination to maintain a show of cool graciousness towards him. Relieved to find that her voice sounded more calm and offhand than she had expected, she said, 'Jim, what on earth are you doing here?'

'I was about to ask *you* the same question,' he answered with the dry amusement she remembered so well.

She disliked the way he had leaned back in his chair as though he was perfectly comfortable and intended staying to talk to her. She felt her inward hostility towards him mounting. He unsettled her more than she cared to admit, and she didn't want him to see it.

'I'm here on holiday,' she replied.

'Alone?' he asked with the merest hint of mockery.

'Yes, at the moment,' she answered. His mockery was not going to goad her into explaining her affairs to him.

'That makes two of us, then,' he answered. 'I've just been concluding a business deal in Naples. I thought while I was in Italy I'd spend a couple of days relaxing before flying home, but I certainly didn't expect to find *you* here.'

Again she thought she detected the edge of dry humour in his tone. Perhaps he did find the irony that they should be staying at the same hotel wryly amusing. But she didn't.

He raised a casual hand and immediately caught the attention of a poolside waiter.

'What will you have to drink?' he asked her as the waiter came over to them.

Alexandra wanted to snap that she wasn't thirsty, but she was too stubborn to let him see she was so on edge. If he could sit here and chat with her as though they had never been joined by anything more than casual acquaintance, then so could she.

'I'll have a Dubonnet and lemonade,' she said.

He ordered a Coke for himself and then turned his attention back to her. His dark eyes raked over her, appreciating her long legs, tanned midriff and the soft swell of her breasts. With his straight black hair and swarthy skin Jim had always reminded her faintly of a buccaneer, and at the moment he was studying her exactly as a pirate might appraise a woman he intended taking for his own. Instinctively her hand went to the gold hoop that fastened her bikini top, making Jim remark lazily, 'Don't worry, everything's in place as it should be.'

His amusement flicked like a whip at her nerves and she said frostily, 'Then maybe you'd be kind enough not to look at me as if you're wondering about including me in your harem.'

'I understand another man's already done that,' he answered.

'My fiancé doesn't have a harem,' she said tartly. 'In any case, how do you . . .?' She broke off as she realised the source of his information. Her grandmother, Ellen, had always got on very well with Jim—so much so that they still kept in touch. Curbing her anger, she went on, but not without a rather obvious defiance. 'So Ellen's told you. Well, yes, as a matter of fact I'm engaged.'

'Congratulations. I hope you'll be very happy.'

The careless generosity of his words made her eyes grow stormy. He didn't know it, but it had been the shattering discovery of his infidelity that had been the cause of her walking out of their foundering two-year-old marriage. For that reason alone it would have given her considerable satisfaction to see that it touched him on the raw that another man had the sense to value what he had thrown away.

'Thank you,' she said coldly. 'I'm sure we will be.'

'Well, don't clam up on me,' drawled Jim. 'What's he like?'

'Roxby's everything you're not, or I wouldn't be marrying him.'

'*Roxby?*'

She glared at him.

'Is there something wrong with the name?'

'No, it's very . . . distinctive. What do you call him, Alex? Rox for short?'

She was finding his derisive humour increasingly hard to take.

'I happen to like the name as it is,' she said shortly. 'Roxby suits him. I don't shorten it, and he doesn't mutilate my name either.'

'So it's Alexandra and Roxby.'

'Yes. The names go together well, and so do we. Perfectly. He's intelligent, considerate, kind . . .'

'Loves children and animals . . .' Jim continued the list in a deft parody before adding, 'All highly desirable qualities.'

'Yes, they are,' she agreed, not pointing out that Roxby didn't score too highly on the last two counts.

'You know, it sounds to me,' remarked Jim, 'as if Roxby will bore you to death with a twelvemonth.'

She should have known he was riling her! Acidly she said, 'I'm really not interested in your opinion of my fiancé. What matters is that he's right for me. He shares my values. You haven't met him . . .'

'You could always arrange it. As someone who knows you quite intimately, I could give him the once-over for you.'

Suddenly and without warning Alexandra's temper snapped.

'You may find this amusing,' she flared, 'but I don't. In fact, I find your presence here extremely aggravating altogether!'

She got to her feet in one taut movement and walked away, too angry to see the glitter in his dark eyes. Damn him and his infuriating mockery!

She stepped on to the tiled edge of the pool, swung

her arms up and dived swiftly and cleanly into the water. Swimming underwater, she emerged some distance from the rail. She must get her emotions under control. Jim didn't mean a thing to her any more, so why was she letting him rile her? She abandoned the question, not wanting to find an answer. Three years ago she had been so determined she would not let him destroy her whole life that she had not even begun to let her feelings surface over his affair with Juliette Stanton. Now, having survived, she would not allow scars she had thought were healed to reopen.

Her breaststroke was graceful and, feeling calmer, she swam a leisurely two lengths. She reached the rail only to see that Jim was standing above her on the tiles. With his feet astride and his arms folded, he seemed menacingly the master of everything he surveyed. And at the moment, as she stood up defensively in the water, he was looking at her. Her eyes went reluctantly to his muscular thighs as he bent down close beside her.

'Can't you leave me alone?' she began, then broke off with a gasp as a powerful hand gripped her by the wrist.

He hauled her out of the water as though she weighed no more than a child, his sinewy arm going round her waist as she stumbled against him. The touch of his honed, mature body made her recoil as if his skin scorched her. Stupefied by his action, she glared up at him, speechless, only to see such a glint of determination in his eyes that her defiance died.

'What . . . what do you want?' she asked a shade breathlessly.

'I haven't finished talking to you yet,' he said, steel behind the easiness.

'I thought everything we had to say to one another was finished three years ago.'

'And finished with quite a degree of civility. So let's

keep it that way, shall we?'

She hadn't heard him use this suppressed tone before that made him sound so dangerous. Jim generally tolerated her waywardness like some amusing prank not worthy of a reprimand. She'd never fully understood how his easy, mocking humour meshed with the signs of forcefulness and purpose in his swarthy face, or the reputation he had in the business world for being as hard as nails.

With him at her side she returned to where they had been sitting. She picked up her towel, drying her face and shoulders, stalling to collect her wits. Suddenly, now that the inexplicable tension between them had ebbed, she couldn't fathom why ever she'd felt so intimidated an instant ago. Her bravado returning, she said, 'Well, you now have my undivided attention. So what is it you want to talk to me about?'

'I'd been meaning to contact you anyway, but now we've met up this is a good chance to get things sorted out.'

She gave him a look of enquiry, not realising how her defensiveness added to her charm, heightening her cameo colouring and deepening the blue of her eyes. Watching her with hawklike keenness, Jim observed drily, 'You haven't lost your old touch, have you?'

'What do you mean?'

'You can still put on the cool-as-hell act that's such a challenge.'

A hot little shiver traced over her skin. Jim was a wolf and she was beginning to feel increasingly unsafe with him. Her heartbeat quickening, she answered, 'I'm really not interested in your opinion of me, shortcomings or otherwise.'

'I didn't say it was a shortcoming, merely that I find it . . . provocative. But before we get sidetracked, let's get back to the question in hand. How's Ellen settling into her new house? It must have been quite a wrench for her moving from Gloucestershire to London.'

The topic was so different from the one she'd been expecting, it took her a minute to reply. She had been braced for a further defence of her fiancé, and now she was almost chagrined with herself for it. How much proof did she need from Jim to see that it meant nothing to him that she was marrying again?

'Yes, I think it was a wrench,' she agreed, telling herself it was a relief to have the conversation on a neutral topic. 'But after that bad fall Ellen had I wasn't happy about her living on her own. Now I think we've got the ideal situation. It was sheer luck the house next door to mine came on the market when it did. Ellen keeps her independence, while I can keep an eye on her.'

'I was sure you'd have her well-being at heart,' he answered. 'In which case, there shouldn't be a problem.'

'A problem about what?' she asked. 'I don't know what you're talking about.'

'I gave Ellen a ring the other day. She happened to mention that her garden was very overgrown, so I said I'd call round to do some cutting back for her. Of course, she was far too tactful to say it in so many words, but it was quite plain that she was worried about accepting my offer in case you objected.'

'That's utter nonsense!' Alexandra retaliated. 'I wouldn't dream of interfering in Ellen's life. In any case, she doesn't need any help in the garden. Yes, it is a bit of a jungle at the moment. The couple who owned the house before loathed gardening. That's why, as soon as I can, I intend getting someone in to start on the heavier cutting back before tidying it up myself.'

'You're missing the point,' said Jim, as though that

was rather to be expected. 'Ellen told me you look in on her every day, but hasn't it occurred to you that away from her old home and most of her friends she might be just a little bit lonely?'

Alexandra drew breath for a denial, and then realised to her annoyance that she was out-argued.

'Listen,' she began, 'as far as I'm concerned you can spend every evening next door, just so long as you keep well away from *me*!'

He gave her a faintly clinical look before commenting, 'What feminine vanity—or were you hoping that after the last time . . .?'

'I wasn't hoping anything,' she snapped, cutting across him. 'That's exactly the sort of cheap, sarcastic quip I'd expect from you. I don't know what came over me that evening. I can only think it was some sort of temporary insanity.'

He saw the angry way she'd blushed, and said as though mocking her was ceasing to amuse him, 'For pete's sake, Alex, keep it in perspective. It was a warm, moonlit night, a wayward moment, and I kissed you.'

'You did more than that!'

He raised a sardonic eyebrow at her accusation, reminding her of her willing co-operation, not needing to have the last word to make his point.

She had driven down to Dursley to spend the weekend with her grandmother. Jim, who had been in the area on business, had happened to call in on the Sunday evening just as she was leaving. But for some reason her car wouldn't start and she was due in court, representing a client, first thing on Monday. Jim had offered her a lift into Gloucester to catch the train.

She was still scorched with the memory of how close they had come to making love in his car. Jim had pulled off the empty country lane because she'd been stupid enough to catch her breath at how beautiful the Severn looked, silvered with moonlight. Her guard had momentarily been down, and when he'd kissed her a treacherous longing had stirred wildly in her blood. When she had finally come to her senses he'd let her fight him off without too much difficulty, but, thinking of his affair with Juliette, she still felt hot with anger and contempt for herself at the way she had behaved.

'I do not wish to discuss what happened the last time I saw you,' she said coldly. 'And neither do I intend sitting here talking to you any longer.'

Jim contemplated her with unfathomable dark eyes.

'I'm sorry,' he replied urbanely, 'I didn't mean to drive you away.'

'You're not driving me away,' she retaliated instantly.

'My mistake,' he said with deft irony as he rested his head back and closed his eyes.

Alexandra glared at him and, with the sole aim of proving him wrong, reached down beside her chair and picked up her paperback. The conversation of the last few minutes had wrecked her concentration but, determined to pretend Jim wasn't there, she struggled on to the end of the chapter.

Finally she flickered a glance at him. He was lying back, his eyes still closed. If he wasn't actually asleep, he was at least dozing, his face in repose, with the play of humour gone from it, as formidably strong as a pirate's. She studied him illicitly, quite proud of her objectivity.

His lashes were black and thick against his swarthy skin, his brows darkly defined and rising outwards from twin creases at the bridge of his nose. With a will of its own her gaze touched the curve of his mouth. Firm and straight, it was as blatantly male as the rest of him. She looked at his strong jaw and felt the startling desire to feel the roughness of his skin beneath her fingers.

The ridiculousness of the impulse amused her, but it was a lonely, wry sort of amusement. She drew a deep breath that was almost a sigh. She could see why she'd once been attracted to Jim. He wasn't conventionally good-looking like Roxby was, but there was a magnetism about him, a sense of determination and even of danger that would appeal to any woman.

Her gaze slipped to his powerful chest, the sight of the dark V of hair making her glance away sharply. She didn't want to remember the feel of his naked body the length of hers, the excitement and tenderness of his passionate lovemaking. A pain surfaced under her ribs, and to her surprise and anger she suddenly felt her eyes burning.

Hurriedly she tucked her head down, forcing her vision to clear till the print came back in focus. She had only just succeeded in taking herself in hand when Jim roused himself to ask lazily, 'So what else is new since I last saw you?'

'I would have thought Ellen would have filled you in with all the details,' she parried, resenting the right he seemed to think he had to know all about her life.

'She said you'd changed jobs,' he answered.

'Yes, I'm working for a firm now that specialises in company law,' she said. 'I moved there just before Christmas. It's where I met my fiancé.'

'So you're still as taken up as ever with your career,' he commented drily.

'Oh?' she flashed back. 'Does it still pique you that I wasn't prepared to sit at home all day, playing wife?'

She wasn't being completely fair to him, considering the support he had given her initially. But she was in no mood to care. It hadn't been her determination to qualify as a solicitor that had broken up their marriage.

'As far as I'm concerned,' he replied a shade harshly, 'it's water under the bridge. I was a fool to think it could work out between you and me in the first place.'

'*You* the fool? No, that was me. I was too blind to even guess . . .'

She broke off abruptly. She wasn't going to fling accusations at him, accusations which at the time she'd been too hurt and too proud to utter.

'Well, luckily this time,' she hurried on, 'I've found everything I've ever wanted in a man. I'm going to build a good marriage, one that's going to last forever, and I'm going to concentrate on being a first-class wife.'

'Don't try too hard,' he advised.

'And what's that supposed to mean?'

'Paragons can be a trial to live with.'

Alexandra bit back a retort before suddenly, in spite of herself, responding to his sense of humour. She was tempted to smile. Then a pang that he had destroyed what they had shared snuffed out completely the amusement in her eyes.

'It's getting late,' she said. 'I think I'll go in and change for dinner.' She got to her feet before he could see that her composure wasn't all that it seemed to be.

The roof of the hotel was divided between the poolside terrace and a small but very pretty garden which the lifts opened on to. A fountain played among a bright mass of geraniums.

Alexandra had only just reached the garden when some instinct told her Jim was following her. She spun round abruptly, whatever she'd been about to say checked as she realised, as he advanced towards her, that in her defensive retreat she had forgotten her book and towel.

'Yours, I believe,' he said as he handed them to her.

His closeness made her feel petite and feminine and much too scantily dressed. Meeting the taunt in his dark eyes, she managed a rather strained, 'Thank you.'

He fell into step beside her. The lift was already waiting, and he stood back so she could enter it ahead of him. Pressing the button for the third floor for himself, he asked, 'Which floor are you on?'

'The same as you,' she answered as the doors slid to.

It was all very well to tell herself that all she had to do was stay calm, treat him with cool civility and the ordeal would soon be over, but it did little to suppress a mounting and inexplicable unease. She had never been as aware of any man physically as she was of Jim. In the confines of the lift she felt almost trapped with him. If only he'd say something to break the curious tension she sensed building up. She kept her eyes fixed on the indicator lights as the lift descended, not daring to so much as glance at him, the pulse that beat at the base of her throat the only visible sign of her agitation.

She was so relieved to arrive at the third floor that she set off along the thickly carpeted corridor ahead of him. It seemed dim after the bright sunlight of the terrace, and his pantherish tread made her feel the need to hurry. There was nothing remotely relaxed in the silence between them, and her heart was starting to beat unevenly.

Glad to reach her room, she quickly put her key in the door. Having opened it, she felt safe enough to turn to Jim to say a cool goodbye. She was just in time to see his gaze lift leisurely, almost insultingly, from the direction of her long legs and trim hips. Immediately she forgot her intention was to be polite and distant with him, and exploded, 'Do you have to look at me like that?'

For once his eyes, implacable and contemptuous, locked with hers without humour. His voice was abrasive as he said, 'You have a very sexy walk, as you very well know, or you wouldn't have minced ahead of me all along the corridor.'

For an instant she stared at him. Then she spluttered, 'You leave me speechless! Do you honestly believe that I have the remotest interest in you . . . that even if I had I'd stoop to . . .? The only thing I feel for you is an immeasurable dislike!'

'That hardly surprises me, since you don't have much regard for men in general. You just like using them.'

'*I don't use people!*' she ground back.

Jim's short laugh had a derisive sound.

'Of course not,' he agreed sarcastically. 'And doubtless your fiancé is a nobody in the firm you work for.'

'He happens to be a senior partner, but don't you *dare* imply . . .'

'That it helps to have someone to pull a few strings for you?' he suggested as he cut across her.

'How I hate you!' she erupted. 'You have a despicable mind. If I've got on, it's because I'm good at my job. Nobody pulls any strings for me—nobody, do you understand? Not even my fiancé.'

'Really?'

The one economical word expressed more derision than Alexandra could have achieved with a whole flow of rhetoric, and as stung as if he had slapped her she said heatedly, 'The biggest mistake I ever made in my life was to marry you, and heaven knows why I did it!'

'Let's try my bank account, for one reason,' answered Jim. He seemed a lot calmer than she, though his jaw was tight and his face as hard as a fist. 'It could stand up to your going to law school when no one else would pick up the bill. Three years on, another man's helping you climb the ladder.'

A sick feeling of disbelief enveloped her. She was scarcely conscious of the pain that slashed at her heart, only of the furious desire to retaliate and hurt him back.

'Well, some men can only get favours from women if they buy them,' she retorted fiercely. 'It seems you're one of them.'

The instant she had spoken she knew she'd gone too far. Jim's eyes glittered ominously as he rasped, '*Am* I?'

He moved with the speed of a hunter, pinning her against the wall with the hardness of his body. Shock made her drop her belongings and, knowing full well his intention, she breathed on a note of panic, 'Jim, don't you dare!'

He didn't answer, and she put up a frightened hand to fend him off. Immediately he snatched hold of it in his vice like grip, while with his other hand he tilted her chin up. She caught a glimpse of his swarthy face, no trace in it now of the man who before had used nothing harsher than the weapon of mockery against her.

'No!' she gasped as he forced her to meet his kiss.

In desperation she grasped hold of his arm, making a muffled sound of protest as she tried to turn her head away.

But her resistance was useless. Jim forced her wrists down, holding them against her sides, and for an instant she stopped fighting him. He had never kissed her like this before. It wasn't brutal, but it was far from gentle, and before she could recover from its devastating, plundering sensuality, his lips parted hers.

He shifted his position, a strong arm going about her waist while his other hand slipped beneath the silky fall of her hair to cradle her head so he could explore her mouth with even greater thoroughness. Hatred of him raged even as she felt a molten fire run like liquid gold through her veins, touching every nerve and cell. A roaring seemed to be filling her ears like the rushing of the sea.

She didn't even realise he was no longer holding her against her will. Her hands came up to steady herself as his kiss deepened. Her bikini was still damp and her nipples tautened in erotic response to the warm hardness of his chest.

His hands slid lower down the length of her spine, and she broke the kiss with a sudden gasp and recoil as his fingers slipped fluently beneath the band of her bikini bottom, pressing her against his aroused body.

She twisted out of his arms, needing the wall behind her for support as she stared up at him with huge dark eyes. For the moment she was so shaken that she scarcely noticed Jim's breathing was as ragged as her own.

'You . . . you bastard!' she breathed.

'You asked for it,' he ground back. Putting a finger to his lips, he touched it lightly to her own as he added with soft derision, 'Besides, you didn't exactly fight me.'

He caught her swinging hand only inches from his face.

'Don't push your luck, Alex,' he said stonily. 'At the time of our divorce I kept my temper with you pretty damn well.'

Alexandra tried to hold his gaze, but his forced hers to drop. Only then did he release his grip on her wrist. She snatched it away and sped inside her room, slamming the door behind her, anger and resentment so fierce inside her that she thought she would choke with it.

CHAPTER TWO

RUBBING her wrist where the red marks from Jim's forceful fingers showed on her fair skin, Alexandra leaned back against the door, her whole body trembling. Her lips still recorded the sensuous pressure of his plundering mouth on hers. With a rare display of tempestuous fury, she hurled her towel on to the bed.

'Damn you, Jim Logan,' she breathed, her voice ragged with suppressed tears. 'Damn you to hell!'

How dared he have kissed her like that, as though he was teaching her a lesson? How *dared* he? Everything that was mettlesome in her rose in rebellion against his male domination. She wasn't good at self-deception, and it fanned the flames of her anger to white heat to know that when he'd tilted her chin up a heady mixture of fear and excitement had raced through her.

She began to pace about. The flagrant injustice of Jim's accusation that she had married him as a means of getting through law school was another knife-thrust of pain and fury. Her eyes began to smart. She had never been impulsive, but she was fiercely tempted to race after him along the corridor and to demand that he take back every contemptuous word.

Instead she crossed the room, flung open the french windows and went out on to the balcony. She stood there, her breathing quickened with her anger. The gossamer-thin net curtains fluttered behind her in the breeze. Beyond the wrought-iron rail of the balcony the bay, lit by the long rays of the sinking sun, was a shimmering expanse of silver. Everything was slowed

25

and made peaceful by the waning radiance which tinted the headlands with lavender tones as they retreated into the distance.

Eyes misted with tears, for a few minutes the tranquillity of the view scarcely impinged on her. Only gradually did it bring to her some measure of calm. She realised she had been holding herself almost rigid, and a small sigh escaped her as her tense shoulders relaxed. Uncrossing her arms, she sat down on the balcony chair.

Jim simply wasn't worth this storm of emotion. The torment he had put her through was over. Why should she try to vindicate herself in a torrent of heated words which would only reveal how totally and deeply she had once loved him? It didn't matter what he thought of her.

The pain lessened as she brought her feelings back under control. But, shocked and bewildered by the explosion of anger and venom between them, she could do nothing to stop herself from trying to account for them. How on earth had it happened, when their divorce had been as clean as an amputation? Even at the end there had been no bitter, violent scenes, no spiteful wrangling over the dividing of their joint assets. Her numbed stoicism had been more than matched by Jim's grim, austere calm.

With growing consternation she realised that among the ashes of their relationship glowed the embers of a sexual chemistry—potent and dangerous enough to lead to the type of grappling that had taken place in the corridor, and perhaps no longer to be masked by polite hostility.

Her heart seemed to jolt with alarm, and as it did so the telephone by her bedside started ringing. She turned her head and stared at it a moment, her mind not attuned to thoughts of her fiancé. Then, as though the phone represented a lifeline to security and sanity, she hurried in from the balcony, tumbling gracefully across the bed as she stretched out her hand to pick up the receiver.

'Hello, darling,' her fiancé began warmly.

'Roxby,' she answered with a breath of laughter, 'it's so good to hear your voice!'

'I like the way you say that,' he teased urbanely. 'It sounds as if you're missing me.'

'I am—more than you could imagine,' said Alexandra, her eyes remote and stormy as she thought of Jim.

'Then I've got news for you that you're going to like,' said Roxby. 'The case will be over tomorrow, so I'll be able to join you at the weekend as planned.'

'That's marvellous! I take it the case has gone well, then.'

'I'd say there's little doubt that we'll get a verdict in our favour,' Roxby said with smooth confidence. 'I think our barrister has established that the employee claiming compensation from his company was drunk at the time of the accident, in which case our clients will be absolved of all responsibility. But anyway, enough about work. Tell me, what have you been doing with yourself today?'

Alexandra's throat tightened without warning. Suddenly she knew she couldn't mention her abominable luck in running into her ex-husband without quite a degree of emotion in her voice. Roxby could easily jump to the wrong conclusion, that she wasn't as over Jim as she appeared to be. It would be more sensible to wait till she was calmer and to tell him about the coincidence when she saw him.

'I've been lazing by the pool mostly,' she answered, her voice a shade constrained. 'Tomorrow I'll probably do some sightseeing.'

'I hope not to Pompeii or Herculaneum,' said Roxby.
'I'm looking forward to showing those to you myself.'

'Not Capri as well?' she asked playfully. 'With the
Blue Grotto, it's supposed to be magical.'

'No, there are too many camera-snapping tourists
there for it to appeal to me,' Roxby answered.

'Well then, perhaps I'll go there tomorrow,' she said.

She and Roxby shared too many interests for it to
matter that their tastes didn't coincide completely. But,
while she did want to visit Capri, at least part of the
island's charm came from knowing that once there she
would be able to relax completely. There would be no
risk of a further turbulent encounter with Jim.

Having enquired about the times of the ferries at
Reception, she decided to catch the eleven o'clock. She
put on a silky sundress in a mixture of pastel colours
which looked good with her lightly tanned skin.
Wanting to feel cool, she decided against bra and
stockings, but in case there was a strong breeze off the
sea she picked up a lightweight jacket.

She glanced at her watch, frowning as she saw that
the hands hadn't moved from when she'd looked at it
before. Realising it must have stopped, she snatched up
her clutch-bag and made briskly for the harbour. The
deep sound of the steamer's siren prompted her to break
into a run, and it was only with a quick sprint that she
reached the gangplank before the sailors hauled it
aboard and cast off.

She went up to the sunny top deck, finding a space at
the rail from which to watch the slowly diminishing
shoreline. She was surprised to find the ferry so
crowded. It wasn't until the Marina Grande at Capri
came into view that she discovered it was the festival of
one of the island's patron saints. The harbour was

decked out with wildly fluttering flags, and she could hear the bells of the *campanile* carrying joyfu ly across the water.

The bus took her up the winding road through vineyards and olive groves to the main town. As Roxby had predicted, it was thronged with tourists, but for Alexandra that merely added to the carnival atmosphere. Music blared as she wandered through the crowded narrow streets with their moulded arches and domes and quaint stairways.

The main square was packed, but she managed to catch a glimpse of the procession as it passed by. The statue of the saint hovered and then moved on, its arms outstretched in blessing as it was paraded on its flower-decked throne high above the crowd.

It was lunchtime before she knew it and, wanting a break from the noise and the bustle, she decided to try the smart but very expensive Terracina Hotel which was noted for its cuisine. She was shown to an open-air table on the spacious terrace which commanded a crow's nest view of the Faraglioni rocks that rose sheer and towering from the dazzling turquoise sea.

Drawn by the breathtaking vista, she set the menu aside and went over to the stone balustrade. The breeze blew a wisp of silky hair loose from her topknot, and she brushed it back, a quality of unconscious grace and freedom about her as she stood gazing out into the distance.

She felt a lot more cheerful than she had last night. Seeing Jim had unsettled her so badly that to avoid meeting him again she'd gone into a restaurant in town. Sitting on her own, she had found it impossible not to start going over the past. Memories of another holiday in Italy had surfaced painfully, together with a host of other recollections of her marriage.

Today it was easier to be positive. It was a long time now since she had cried over Jim, a long time since she'd woken sobbing and breathless from a nightmare made up of vivid cameos of their break-up. About to start a new life with Roxby, she had no reason any longer to feel depressed about the failure of her marriage to Jim.

Absorbed, she didn't hear a man's lithe footfall, and the firm hand at her elbow startled her. She turned unsuspectingly, almost to collide with Jim's chest. Her senses shrilled alarm at the contact, and she recoiled so sharply that he had to steady her. His fingers bit into her arm as he said, aggression beneath the mockery, 'Are you following me, Alex?'

She pushed his hand away as though his touch burned her. The air was as full of agitation and electricity as it had been yesterday. Her heart was beating far too quickly and unevenly, but she managed to retort, 'I'm doing anything *but* following you!'

Amused comprehension came into the dark eyes that pinned hers, and she coloured at how stupidly she had given herself away. The austerity had gone from Jim's face as he remarked, 'So you thought you'd visit Capri to avoid me.'

'That was one of the reasons, yes,' she answered with cold hostility.

His virile masculinity made her feel breathless, but she would not take a step backwards. She forced herself to stand her ground and meet his eyes.

'I'm glad it wasn't the only reason, or you'd have done better to have stayed put,' he said, before explaining. 'I checked out of the hotel in Sorrento this morning. I'm spending the next two days here before flying back to London.'

'Well, luckily this isn't the only hotel on the island,' snapped Alexandra. 'I'll find somewhere else to eat.'

She went to walk past him. Just the sight of him was enough to shatter her poise, stirring her with that mixture of anger and excitement, panic and defiance which she couldn't begin to analyse.

With lightning reflexes Jim snatched hold of her wrist, stopping her from leaving. His brows were drawn together with impatience as he snapped, 'For pity's sake, Alex, stop acting like a child! You can't be as nervous of me as this.'

'I'm not nervous of you at all,' she lied. 'But after the way you behaved yesterday, are you really surprised that I'd rather be anywhere than standing here talking to you?'

'In which case, I'll apologise. I've no wish to spoil your day.'

Without meaning to, Alexandra spoke the thought aloud. 'Spoil my day? You had a damn good shot at spoiling my whole life!'

Jim paused before answering. Then, his temper in check, he said with abrasive sarcasm, 'I know being in court has given you a flair for the dramatic, but isn't that a little over the top? As I remember, I didn't stop you from doing anything you wanted the whole time we were married.'

'Maybe . . .' She choked off the rest of her remark.

'Maybe *what*?' he demanded incisively.

'Maybe nothing,' she said, throwing the words at him.

Turning sharply to hide the angry tears in her eyes, she left the terrace, taking the shortest escape by means of the steps down to the gardens.

She walked quickly, rejoining the road, not caring which streets she took as long as the general direction was away from the Terracina Hotel. Why was she finding it impossible suddenly to stop Jim from

shattering her defences? She thought she'd dealt with all
her feelings for him. Hurriedly she dismissed the notion.
She *had* dealt with her feelings for him. It was merely
that he had caught her off balance. If she'd had warning
that she had been going to meet him again, neither the
scene just now nor the one the previous evening would
have happened.

She found a pretty rustic-style restaurant where she
sat out under a vine-covered pergola, but the encounter
with Jim seemed to have taken away her appetite. It was
only as she came to pay the bill that she realised that in
any event it was just as well that she hadn't had lunch at
the Terracina. She didn't have as much money on her as
she'd thought. There had been a couple of incidents of
bag-snatching in Sorrento, and she'd left her credit
cards and traveller's cheques in her room the previous
evening before she'd gone into the town. In her hurry to
catch the ferry this morning, she had evidently forgotten
to slip them back in her bag.

Returning to the main square, she debated how to
spend the afternoon. She wasn't likely to bump into Jim
again, and anyway, she refused to let him influence her
plans any longer. A fresh breeze had got up and the sea
was too choppy for the boat trips to the Blue Grotto to
be running.

But there were other treasures to see, and by the time
she had visited the Villa San Michele it was getting late.
She touched the granite sphinx that gazed out
imperiously over the sea from the gardens, then smiled
at herself for half believing the superstition. As Capri
didn't appeal to Roxby, it wasn't likely that some day
she would come back.

The last ferry was due to sail at just before six.
Alexandra was a shade surprised as she got down from
the bus to see that the steamer wasn't already in the

harbour. The oleanders tossed in the wind and the brooding sky showed that there would be a storm before long. She would have liked the ferry to have got away on time before the sea became any rougher.

The deteriorating weather meant that the hydrofoil had been cancelled—she supposed that accounted for the crowd of people. Yet it didn't explain the hubbub of noise and confusion, nor the uniformed official she could see waving his arms and talking volubly in Italian.

People began to detach themselves from the throng and to head back towards the waiting buses. Starting to get worried, Alexandra seized her chance to catch the attention of one of the officials.

'Can you tell me what's happening?' she began anxiously.

'The ferry, it's not running,' he answered in strongly accented English. Pointing to the buses, he went on, 'You go back to town now and come here tomorrow.'

'Not running?' she exclaimed. 'But why?'

'Engine trouble. That's why everyone goes back into town.'

'You mean I've got to spend the night here?' she said, thinking frantically of how little money she had.

The official shrugged, gave her a harassed apology and moved on. He was having to deal with passengers far more put-out than she.

The only thing to do was to try and book in somewhere as cheaply as she could. There was no point wishing she'd caught an earlier ferry, or in visualising her room back at the hotel, her nightgown and her toiletries all to hand.

Her sensible attitude lasted well until the second hotel she tried told her it had no vacancies. By now the dusk was falling fast. The swaying cypresses heralded the first heavy drops of thunder rain. She didn't want to ask Jim

to lend her some money, but stubborn pride wasn't
going to get her very far when it came to finding a room
for the night.

Tiredly she started towards the Terracina. As she
neared it the storm broke, forcing her to run the last
part of the way. She paused in the lobby to catch her
breath.

The atmosphere of understated elegance and
responsive service made her feel like a bedraggled
intruder. Light sparkled from the three Venetian glass
chandeliers and gleamed on the marble pillars. Against
the wall, vases massed with flowers had their beauty
reflected by huge gilt-framed mirrors. The deep
armchairs looked comfortable and yet made little
impact on the spaciousness of the lobby.

A *soignée*, dark-haired woman was on duty behind
the reception desk. She glanced up enquiringly as
Alexandra approached, and asked, 'Can I help you?'

'Yes. You have a Mr Jim Logan staying here. Would
you tell him Ms Challoner would like to speak to him?'

The woman's well-manicured hand went to the
telephone. Then she stopped, her dark eyes looking
beyond Alexandra as she said, 'There's Mr Logan
coming across the lobby now.'

Alexandra turned quickly. Jim, arrestingly urbane in
white shirt and dinner-jacket, was heading in her
direction. From the impact he made on her, this might
have been the first time she had seen him in evening
dress. The precision tailoring and the austere blackness
of the material gave a disturbing impression of latent
strength, of an edge of ruthlessness dormant behind the
suave façade. His was the sexual magnetism of virility,
success and power.

He spotted her immediately. Trying to give the
impression of composure, Alexandra walked towards

him.

'It's an old line,' he quipped, 'but you and I are going to have to stop meeting like this.'

She was acutely conscious of how untidy she looked. The skirt of her dress was splashed with rain from the downpour, and her topknot was coming loose. Furthermore, she knew from Jim's masculine gaze that not one detail of her appearance had passed him unnoticed.

'I'm not in the mood for your sense of humour,' she snapped.

'You used to have one yourself,' he answered. 'Roxby seems to have killed off your *joie de vivre.*'

'I didn't come here to discuss my fiancé with you,' she said shortly.

'Don't tell me,' he said lazily. 'You've missed the last steamer. That wasn't very clever of you.'

'I didn't miss it,' she corrected him coldly. 'It's not running. It's in Sorrento harbour with engine trouble.'

Tired and frustrated and at a disadvantage with Jim, she knew it wouldn't take much more for her to burst into tears. There had been an unmistakable catch in her voice and, determined to conceal it, she went on with a rush of antagonism, 'Which is why I haven't got the time or the patience to stand here matching words with you. I want to book in somewhere for the night, but I haven't got much money on me. I was hoping you'd lend me some.'

'I'll lend you some, of course. But if you're about to try a less expensive hotel you'll find it's as full as this one. With the festival, everywhere's booked up.'

His kinder tone, when she knew his opinion of her, was somehow infinitely harder to endure than his dry sarcasm. She retorted sharply, 'Thank you so much for pointing out the obvious!'

A smile twitched at the corners of his attractive mouth.

'Well, *as* it's the obvious,' he said with deft irony, 'what exactly are you planning to do?'

'You needn't worry about me. Just lend me some money and I'll find somewhere to spend the night.'

'The street?' he suggested, before adding, 'For once, put your pride in your pocket, Alex. You can share my room.'

'Share your room?' she repeated, astounded. 'Are you joking? Believe me, I'd *sooner* sleep on the street!'

'Don't be ridiculous,' he cut across her, the humour stripped from his voice. 'Do you really think I'm going to let you walk out of here with nowhere to stay?'

'And do you think *I'm* going to let you smuggle me into your room like some . . . like some . . .'

'Courtesan?' Jim supplied mockingly. She coloured and he went on, 'That wasn't my intention. Wait here and I'll get things sorted out.'

She wasn't sure if it was the authority in his manner or the fact that she felt too defeated to argue, but she made no attempt to assert her independence. As he strode off to the reception desk she sank into one of the gold brocade armchairs.

For an instant she felt almost relieved that he'd taken charge, and then dismay enveloped her. What was she thinking of? Roxby aside, she couldn't share a bedroom with her ex-husband. She looked at the plate-glass doors with the half-formed intention of running off into the night.

The sight of the teeming rain, slanting in the lights from the hotel, stopped her. Beyond was a mystery of blackness, illuminated occasionally by a vivid flash of blue-white lightning. She'd be soaked to the skin in seconds if she went out into the storm.

Almost without realising it she settled back into the warm comfort of the armchair. She forced herself to be rational. She was perfectly safe from Jim as long as she kept her head. In fact, she ought to be grateful to him for having helped her out.

She glanced at him. He was being dealt with immediately at the reception desk, the woman's rather immobile face suddenly full of smiling charm.

Alexandra looked away. His curt protectiveness towards her filled her with a strange mixture of indignation and bleakness. She might be over him, but although it was completely illogical she didn't want him to be over her. Yet it was quite clear that he was, apart from the fact that she still interested him sexually. The thought was alarming and she swiftly abandoned it.

Jim was soon back.

'Well, that's all settled,' he said as he sat down in an armchair beside her.

'How . . . how exactly did you explain it?' she ventured.

Jim leant back comfortably. It crossed her mind that the relaxation of his body was reminiscent of a panther at rest. His immaculate appearance only made him seem more dangerously male.

'The Italians are very understanding when it comes to affairs of the heart,' he said. 'I explained that you're my ex-wife and that you'd followed me here with a reconciliation in mind. I think the woman at the desk was quite touched.'

'You didn't!' she exclaimed furiously, seeing too late the amusement in his eyes. The realisation that he was merely trying to get a rise out of her made her explode. 'I don't have to take this!'

His hand on her arm stopped her from getting up. His grasp was like a charge of electricity, and it momentarily knocked the fight out of her.

'What are you thinking of?' he asked. 'Walking out of here? Perhaps you're not aware of it, but the Italian police are quite zealous in rounding up ladies of the night, and I'd hate you to be mistaken for one of them. I know your lawyer fiancé could always arrange bail and vouch for your character . . .' He laughed at the murderous expression in her eyes and said, 'Simmer down, Alex. It's been unfortunate that you've got stranded here, and I realise that you have your reputation to think of, but you'll survive a night in my company. Now, have you had dinner?'

She forced herself to check her temper. Indebted to him, she was in no position to reject the olive branch he was offering.

'No, no, I haven't,' she answered more amenably. 'But I'd like to neaten up a bit first.'

Jim felt in his jacket pocket for his key, and said as he handed it to her, 'My room's on the second floor. I'll meet you down here when you're ready.'

She accepted the key and crossed the lobby to the regal marble staircase. For a moment he'd treated her so much as though they were still married that she felt hopelessly confused. A curious wistfulness tugged at her heart, which she dismissed impatiently. She was tired and her resistance was low, that was all it was. Emotionally she was still completely in control.

She let herself into Jim's room and switched on the light. Luxuriously furnished, it was dominated by a double bed. She stared at it, her heartbeat beginning to skip with near-panic. Quickly she took herself in hand and glanced about. The Empire-style sofa didn't look any more comfortable to sleep on than the elegant armchairs. But it was only for one night, and it would have to do.

She felt too much of a trespasser to draw the striped curtains which fell in smooth pleats from the corniced ceiling to the thick-piled carpet. Instead she slipped off her jacket and went into the opulently appointed bathroom. Clean towels were in abundance, and she looked longingly at the shower, but thought she had better not keep Jim waiting. He might come up to see what was taking her so long, and she had no wish to be caught with no clothes on.

She opened her bag to find her lipstick and mascara. She felt a stab of annoyance with herself for having three lipsticks to choose from when she'd forgotten her credit cards. But just the same she was glad she had her atomiser of Rive Gauche. Its fragrance boosted her morale.

She couldn't re-do her topknot with only a comb, but she hesitated before picking up Jim's hairbrush. Using his belongings was a poignant reminder of the intimacy of marriage.

She glanced at her reflection. Luckily her sundress was chic, so that she wouldn't look too out of place in the dining-room where everyone would be in evening clothes. Her topknot was smooth and severe and her eyes a deep, clear blue. Only the slight flush of her cheeks betrayed her. Not wanting to work out why a man who had no relevance in her life could unsettle her so, she returned to Jim in the lobby.

He got to his feet as she approached, and she tried not to be aware of how devastatingly attractive he looked. His white shirt emphasised the piratical swarthiness of his skin, while the fit of his dinner-jacket enhanced his lean, muscular build. Somehow he conveyed the impression of gentlemanliness and danger at the same time.

She hunted for something to say, wanting to dispel

the panicky feeling that she was out of her depth. But, conscious of his dark eyes looking her over, her mind seemed to go blank.

'Why the chignon?' he asked. 'I always preferred you with your hair loose.'

Alexandra had meant not to be antagonistic, but with his proprietorial remark the resolution vanished immediately.

'How you preferred my hair is no affair of yours any longer, now is it?' she answered.

'I wouldn't say that,' Jim commented lazily as, putting a hand at her elbow, he guided her in the direction of the dimly lit Marquis dining-room. '"A thing of beauty is a joy for ever." And I never tired of enjoying you!'

His deliberate reference to their more intimate moments made her fingers itch to slap him. Against her will she remembered the feel of his hand smoothing her wildly tumbled hair after they had made love. Yet he'd obviously enjoyed his nights with Juliette far more than any of those he'd spent with her. Despite the demon of jealousy that raged inside her, she managed to reply coldly, 'I'm too old to wear my hair loose down my back.'

'You're still a young woman,' Jim answered, adding, 'Besides, with eyes like that you'll never be old.'

Taking their seats at one of the secluded tables interrupted their conversation. Alexandra waited till the waiter moved away. Then, meeting Jim's eyes without a flicker of anything other than chilly hauteur, she asked levelly, 'Are you flirting with me, Jim?'

She congratulated herself both on the remark and on her delivery of it. Now he would see just how little he affected her. But the sense of satisfaction was shortlived. His gaze held hers, and the sardonic glitter she saw there made her heart start to race with a senseless apprehension.

'Why?' he answered softly. 'Would you like me to?'

'No, I would not,' she retorted. 'In case you've forgotten, I happen to be engaged.'

'To a man who's . . . What were those sterling qualities you listed? Well, whatever they were, it seems Roxby's not the man you need.'

'What do you mean?' Alexandra fired back.

'I mean, if he was man enough to satisfy you in bed, you wouldn't still be flashing fire and sending me sexual signals a man could read a mile off.'

'How dare you?' she breathed with concentrated fury.

'Believe me,' he answered abrasively, 'I dare plenty.'

She knew instinctively that to retaliate or to push him any further was simply asking for trouble. Normally, common sense would have stopped her. Now, she seemed beyond the reach of caution.

'Try it and see where it gets you!' she snapped heatedly.

Suddenly there was so much static between them, she thought the air must snap with it. For a terrifying instant she was certain she'd gone too far. Jim's dark eyes glittered as they pierced hers. The racking moment dragged on, and then he said, menace in the lazy quietness of his voice, 'Let me tell you something as an old friend. Never issue a man with that kind of challenge unless you're prepared to take the consequences.'

A hot little shiver ran over her skin. Her mouth felt dry as she dragged her gaze away from his, incapable of an answer. She was thankful for the waiter who came up to ask solicitously if they were ready to order, and she nodded when Jim suggested that he decide for them both.

Trying hard to rally, she looked round at her surroundings while Jim spoke to the waiter. The high-backed, red-upholstered chairs were so arranged that till now she'd scarcely been aware of the other diners. She and Jim might have been alone in a setting as rich as Aladdin's cave.

She glanced at the singer who was at the microphone with the band at the end of the dance-floor. Her silver and white dress gleamed in the muted lighting, and as Alexandra watched she moved to drape an arm idly along the grand piano. Her husky voice matched perfectly with the soft, insinuating music.

To Alexandra the whole ambience seemed to be conspiring against her in her attempt to keep her emotions firmly in check. Her fingers went to touch the back of her chignon, an unconscious gesture she tended to make when life was particularly taxing. It was only just after nine o'clock, she thought in alarm. She had the whole night ahead of her to get through.

Yet unexpectedly Jim took the pressure off her throughout the meal. He kept the conversation light, and gradually she relaxed with him. She had forgotten how his sense of humour could disarm her. Yet, although she smiled and came back with quick remarks, her eyes remained wary. Jim might have damped down the static between them, but some strange intuition warned her that it wouldn't take much for it to surface again.

As they lingered over coffee and liqueurs she found herself studying him. If only she'd known from the start that despite the rapport between them Jim wasn't the right partner for her. He would have been ideal if all she'd wanted was some breathless, exciting love-affair, but, with the sort of charisma that meant he could charm any woman he desired, he wasn't the type to settle down. Before she could feel the sharp tug of regret she remarked, 'You must have been very pleased to have your company receive one of the Queen's Awards for Industry this year.'

'I didn't realise you were still interested enough to follow the affairs of Global Freightways,' answered Jim, his brows coming together quizzically.

'I happened to read it in the newspaper,' she told him, not letting his mockery ruffle her. 'It's been hard to avoid articles on your current expansion.'

There was a short pause. Then he said, a note of harshness in his voice, despite the apparent casualness of his reply, 'Well, for a while I thought of little else.'

Her eyes flew to his, her gaze dropping as pain twisted at her heart.

Work wasn't a cure for the agony of loss, as she knew, but it helped. What had caused Jim's relationship with Juliette to end and meant that he'd put all his energy into his company? She had obviously been the reason why he'd made no attempt to save his marriage. Alexandra had assumed he'd welcomed the chance to be free.

Yet six months later Juliette had given up her job as his secretary, moved to the Hull branch of his company and the affair was presumably over. Even with some artfully artless questions, Alexandra hadn't been able to determine which one of them had made the break. It seemed she would never know, and for that reason alone she would always wonder what Juliette had meant to him, what she had been able to give him that must have been lacking in their own relationship.

She fingered the rim of her coffee-cup, not sensing immediately Jim's dark gaze on her.

'Why so quiet all of a sudden?' he asked.

'I . . . I was thinking,' she stalled.

'What about?'

'About how I'm going to explain this to Roxby, for one,' she said, her tone implying that the whole situation was somehow Jim's fault.

'You don't need to explain it to him,' Jim answered. 'It's perfectly innocent, and anyway, you know what they say. What the eye doesn't see, the heart doesn't grieve over.'

'Yes, that's always been your motto, hasn't it?' Alexandra retorted with a touch of venom.

His eyes narrowed on her. As though he was weighing his answer, he said, 'I've never believed in upsetting anyone unnecessarily.'

'I'm different,' she said with hostility. 'I happen to like a relationship based on total honesty and total trust.'

Jim shrugged slightly as though that was up to her. Then he said with the amusement that left her so helpless to retaliate, 'Well, whatever story you decide to give to Roxby when you see him, I'll back you up.'

'You won't have to back me up. One thing my fiancé knows he'll never have to accuse me of is infidelity. When I choose a partner I stick to him.'

'Good for you,' Jim answered.

He obviously felt not the slightest stab of guilt over his affair. Rather she had the infuriating comprehension that he was finding her not only entertaining, but a challenge that he was more and more inclined to take on. The suspicion was confirmed when he asked, 'Which would you prefer, to dance or to have an early night?'

In normal circumstances she would have snapped 'Neither!' She would have liked to have put him down by telling him she didn't wish to dance, but the thought of being confined with him in that stately blue and cream bedroom was beginning to haunt her. Besides, she wasn't going to let him see he had got her on the run.

She was twenty-nine years old, a woman who'd survived the trauma of a divorce. Surely she had the confidence and maturity to deal with both Jim and the situation?

'Yes, I'd like to dance,' she announced with a touch of defiance.

'Good,' answered Jim.

He stood back, allowing her to precede him on to the intimate dance-floor where in the romantic shadows several couples were moving to the sentimental music. Continuing with her bravado, she put her hands up to rest on Jim's broad shoulders, despite the fact that her heart had begun to clamour wildly, a reflex reaction to his nearness that she could do nothing about.

Jim drew her closer so that their bodies fitted together perfectly. His hand was warm against her back, and suddenly, aware of him in every nerve, Alexandra felt herself stiffen and start to tremble.

'It's . . . it's so long since I've danced, I seem to have lost the knack,' she lied, hoping her voice sounded less nervous to his ears than it did to her own.

'It'll come back,' he murmured.

She realised she should never have started this dangerous game of trying to convince him of her complete invulnerability. Already she could sense his tremendous magnetism beginning to mesmerise her, some wild homing instinct making a shiver run through her. It took all her self-control not to pull away in panic, but to stay in his arms till the number ended.

Joining in the clapping, she said hurriedly, 'I'd rather not dance any more. It's been a long day and I'm tired.'

'I take it, then, you're ready for bed.'

There was just the right degree of provocation in his tone to shatter their temporary truce. Glaring up at him, she retorted, 'Not ready for bed, Jim. *I'm* sleeping on the sofa.'

CHAPTER THREE

WITH a hand at her elbow, Jim escorted her from the dance-floor.

'Now that's a shame,' he drawled, 'because I was rather looking forward to tucking you up in that king-sized bed.'

'Yes, I bet you were,' she said with hostility, her pulse quickening. 'If you thought for one minute that I'd consent to sleep . . . to share a bed with you, you must be crazy!'

'Who said anything about sharing a bed?' he asked mockingly.

'*You* just did.'

'Oh, no, I didn't,' he corrected her. 'I was very chivalrously offering to tuck you up alone in it. Somehow you misunderstood me. But perhaps the wish was father to the thought.'

Alexandra turned on him with a surge of anger.

'Now, let's get one thing straight,' she flashed back. 'I have no desire to . . .'

Her voice failed her. Somehow she couldn't complete the intimate sentence when Jim's dark eyes had ensnared hers. A strange electricity flickered along her nerves. Together with her inability to hold his gaze, it increased her temper and, as they continued on their way out of the dining-room, she said in a chilly undertone, 'I know you have a strong sex drive, but do you think we could eliminate bed from the conversation?'

'I didn't realise you found the subject of where you're

going to sleep tonight so . . . threatening.'

'I don't find sex or you threatening,' she snapped.

'You know, your mind seems to be running on sex tonight,' observed Jim as they crossed the elegant lobby. 'For someone who says they want to leave the subject alone, you're bringing it into every sentence.'

'I most certainly am not,' she retaliated, annoyed with herself the instant she'd spoken.

She ought to have ignored his comment, not taken him up on it. Somehow it seemed impossible for her to stop sparring with him, even though their conversation was making her more flustered by the minute. Determined to recover her composure, she went on coldly, 'My only concern is how I'm going to manage for the night on the sofa.'

'Some people could manage on the sofa very well,' Jim said with a glint of amusement.

'That's not funny!' she erupted, her eyes blazing.

He caught hold of her arm with sudden annoyance.

'Are you really so tense you can't even recognise a joke?' he demanded curtly.

'I don't call that a joke,' she retorted.

He allowed her to maintain a stony silence with him as they went up the staircase. It wasn't until they had reached the door to his room that he swung her towards him. She gave a timid gasp, making his brows come together more sternly still.

'Now listen,' he began with quiet ferocity, 'I'm getting a little tired of your acting in this high-strung manner with me.'

'I'm not acting in a high-strung manner,' she lied.

'No?' he queried, letting his hands slide caressingly up her bare arms.

Recoiling as though his touch burned her, Alexandra hissed, 'Don't you dare touch me like that!'

He pulled her to his chest, every vestige of humour gone from his eyes.

'Maybe it's time I set your mind at rest,' he said gratingly. 'Attractive though you are, I'm not so highly sexed nor so starved of women's company that the moment we're behind that door I'm going to throw you on the bed and ravish you. I take it from your reaction just now that *is* what's troubling you?'

She blushed hotly and stumbled unsuccessfully for an answer. Jim watched her, a smile that had little to do with amusement lifting the corners of his mouth. Releasing her abruptly, he went on, 'So now you have my assurance that the only way things will hot up between us tonight is by your invitation . . .'

'You'll wait for ever for that!' she interrupted angrily.

'In which case,' he replied sarcastically as he unlocked the door, 'perhaps you'll calm down.'

She gave him a glacial stare.

'I *am* calm,' she answered with a steadiness that would have been perfect, if only it had matched her heartbeat.

Determined to live up to her statement, Alexandra went ahead of him into the bedroom—only to realise how acutely out of place and endangered she felt. She stood irresolute at the foot of the bed, fidgeting with her clutch-bag.

Jim came towards her, took it out of her hands in one firm gesture and threw it carelessly into an armchair.

'Relax, Alex. You're not caged with a tiger.' His voice had an edge. He was obviously out of patience with her.

'The name's Alexandra,' she reminded him as she sat down gingerly on the edge of the bed.

'Old habits die hard,' he replied drily.

He moved to draw the curtains. Their rasp covered
the soft beat of the incessant downpour. She crossed her
legs and nervously swung her downward-pointing foot.
Now that the curtains were across she felt even more
shut in with him. Swiftly she stood up and switched on
the radio. Anything would be better than a lengthening
silence.

'What's this a sign of?' asked Jim, the inevitable
humour back in his tone. 'Do you want to go on
dancing?'

'No, I just don't like it so quiet, that's all.'

'Perhaps you'd like the TV on, then?' he mocked.
'Pictures as well as sound. You'd feel less alone with
me.'

'It doesn't worry me being alone with you,' she said,
her eyes clashing with his. 'Undoubtedly you'd like it to,
but you've meant nothing to me for the last three years.'

'In which case there need be no tension.'

As he spoke he pulled his bow-tie undone and took
off his jacket. Alexandra watched, disturbed and yet
fascinated by his movements, by the muscles she saw
ripple under his pristine white shirt. All evening she had
been intrigued by the contrast between his urbane attire
and his virile masculinity.

He sat down in an armchair and undid his collar. For
a mad instant she pictured herself unfastening his shirt
for him, her fingers playing down till she had opened
every button. He glanced up, and the piercing directness
of his dark eyes made her realise how avidly she had
been staring. Apparently unconcerned, he pulled his
shirt off. The gleaming power of his broad shoulders
and sinewy arms galvanised her into action. Heavens,
he'd be taking his trousers off next!

'I . . . I think I'll take a shower,' she announced
quickly.

Jim laughed, and she knew that if he hadn't read her every thought he'd at least come close to the last one.

'Fine,' he answered. 'Do you need any help?'

'I'm quite capable of showering by myself, thank you,' she answered shortly.

'Pity,' he commented.

She escaped into the bathroom, closed the door and leaned against it. Gradually her breathing became more regular and her pulse-rate slowed down. But her eyes remained stormy. She hated him for the easy, relaxed way he could behave with her. Maybe he was even getting a kick out of discomforting her. Believing it would have helped justify her anger, except she knew it wasn't true. Jim was merely carrying on as if she wasn't there.

She showered and had just wrapped one of the large towels around her sarong-fashion when it occurred to her that she had nothing to put on. She hesitated a moment and then opened the door, her voice admirably even as she called, 'Jim?'

'Yes?'

'Do you have a shirt I could wear to sleep in?'

'I'll find one for you.'

She hovered in the doorway, hearing him go to the chest of drawers. A minute later he came into her range of vision. She saw his eyes travel in appreciative male scrutiny over her bare shoulders that still glistened with the last drops of the shower that she had neglected to dry off.

'If only you'd drop the towel, you'd make as lovely a sight as Venus rising from the waves,' he commented lazily.

'I have no intention of dropping the towel,' she said frostily. The gleam in his eyes was making her skin tingle. 'Now, would you please hand me the shirt?'

He held it out to her and, snatching hold of it, Alexandra ducked back into the bathroom. The cuffs came well over her wrists and she pushed them up, seeing in the mirror how his shirt emphasised her femininity. Deep down, was she as vulnerable as she looked? She dismissed the ridiculous question. She'd have to get a grip on herself.

While Jim took his turn in the bathroom, she made up her makeshift bed, glad of something to do. She borrowed one of his pillows and found a spare blanket on a shelf in the wardrobe.

Going to the window, she pulled the curtain aside and looked out. The darkness was almost complete. Raindrops clung to the glass, and as she stood there she heard more strike it lightly. One thing was certain—she'd had no choice but to accept Jim's hospitality.

She settled down on the sofa and pulled the blanket over her legs. She had just begun to unpin her hair when Jim joined her. Seeing his naked muscular legs beneath his navy silk dressing-gown, she remembered with a little jittery flutter that when it was hot Jim didn't bother with pyjamas.

'So you really meant it when you said you were going to curl up on the sofa,' he commented.

'Your offer was appreciated,' she said, striving to keep her voice detached, 'but there's no way all six foot two of you would fit on here.'

'You could be right,' he agreed as he switched off the main light, leaving only the gentle glow from the table-lamp by the bed. Turning back the covers, he went on, 'Well, if you change your mind, or get lonely in the night, you have a standing invitation to come and snuggle up beside me.'

Alexandra checked her reply, seeing him untie his

belt. Hurriedly averting her eyes, she made a great show of running her fingers through the curtain of her hair in search of stray pins, his discreetness as he discarded his dressing-gown lost on her. Somehow she didn't feel strong enough to see him dominant and magnificently naked.

When she dared glance up he was in bed, reaching over to pick up the sheet of card that lay beside the table-lamp. Its glow sculptured his face in light and shadow, the strong planes of his cheek and brow, the determined jaw. For some reason she couldn't seem to keep her eyes from him.

Studying the card, his ballpoint in his hand, he asked, 'Tea or coffee in the morning? And do you want a full cooked breakfast, bacon, eggs, sausages . . .'

'I shall leave before breakfast,' she interrupted.

'Do you have to be unnecessarily difficult,' he asked, looking up with a frown. 'I appreciate that you want to catch an early ferry, but you're not leaving here without something to eat, and they serve breakfast in the room from six o'clock onwards.'

'When are you going to stop ordering me about?'

'Perhaps when you stop behaving like a truculent ten-year-old. Now, what are you going to have, a cooked breakfast or coffee and croissants?'

'And I suppose if I say neither, you'll force-feed me,' said Alexandra, capitulating with bad grace. 'All right, then, coffee and croissants.''

'Fine,' said Jim, his expression grimly good-humoured as he added an extra tick to the list.

His hand went to the covers. Her assumption that he was about to get out of bed with the card made her act with an impetuousness that took him by surprise. Almost tripping over her blanket in her haste, she stumbled to her feet, snatched the card from him and fled across the room to hang it outside on the doorknob.

As she returned to the sofa she was aware of his highly amused smile. It did nothing for her temper. She said coldly, 'I'm ready for the light to go out now.'

He reached across and switched it off, plunging the room in darkness.

'You still haven't told me what you're doing in Sorrento on your own,' he said. 'What's happened to Roxby?'

She wasn't sure which she disliked more, the infuriating mild jeer he managed to put into her fiancé's name, or the darkness that heightened the suffocating intimacy of the night. Refusing to let annoyance show in her voice, she said, 'He had to be in court this week. He's joining me tomorrow afternoon.'

'So he puts work before taking a holiday with you. That doesn't augur too well for your future.'

'You don't have to live in someone's pocket in order to have a good relationship,' she told him. 'In any case, it's got nothing to do with you.'

'I wouldn't say that.'

'What do you mean?'

'You were my wife for two years. It's only to be expected I still take some interest in you,' Jim said carelessly.

'A proprietorial interest?' she asked, all the more acidly because of the absurd way her heart had leapt an instant ago.

Jim's voice took on an abrasive intonation.

'If I'd looked on you as some kind of possession, I wouldn't have let you divorce me.'

A sense of underlying danger flared in the dark. A few more incautious words on her part, and the façade of distant friendliness between them would start to shatter. The knowledge of it made her change the subject quickly and say, 'You haven't told me what you're doing here, either.'

'I thought I had,' he remarked, before explaining, 'I flew into Naples on business. As you know, I've always liked Italy, so I thought I'd have a few days' holiday while I was here.'

'Alone?' she said, her tone more antagonistic and sceptical than she had intended.

'Yes, alone,' he replied caustically. 'Contrary to what you seem to think, I can survive without a woman for short intervals.'

'I don't remember ever seeing much evidence of that!' she muttered.

'Alex, don't provoke me any more,' he said gently. 'You'll regret it. Now go to sleep.'

Her instinct was to retaliate. It was the strange sensual shiver along her spine that stopped her. Annoyed that with such a soft tone Jim could have cowed her, she thumped the pillow into shape and didn't answer.

The silence lengthened. How was it, she wondered with angry puzzlement, that Jim could stir up in her such volatile rage and burning resentment? She couldn't seem to stop herself deliberately setting a match to the tinder-box atmosphere between them, and yet if there was one thing she hated, it was heated, emotional scenes. She'd witnessed enough of those between her parents as a child at home.

Partly why she so appreciated Roxby was because they didn't strike sparks off each other. In all the time she'd known him they had not once had a fight of any kind. Yet for once thoughts of her fiancé weren't enough to curb her restlessness. Sleep was obviously going to elude her.

Not so Jim. She listened to the sound of his deep,

even breathing. She thought she could see the rise and fall of his chest, but in the enveloping dark she wasn't sure. The covers were tangled roughly round his waist as he lay completely relaxed, one swarthy arm flung upwards on the pillow.

She bit her lip, conscious of a weak desire to cry which she would not give in to. She had never thought when she had married Jim that five years on they would share a hotel bedroom as total strangers.

Her eyes held the quiet brightness of unshed tears, as, unable to help herself, she thought back to her wedding day. She had been so in love, so certain that everything would always be as beautiful as the day itself.

Yet initially her background had made her extremely marriage-shy. A father whom she hadn't heard from since she was ten, and a mother who married at the drop of a hat, hadn't given her much confidence in the institution. Subconsciously she made the decision that it was best to love lightly. That way she couldn't get hurt. And the fact that as soon as a relationship with a boyfriend became serious it for one reason or another broke up only confirmed her opinion that most men were, like her father, unreliable.

In any case, her main concern was qualifying as a solicitor. She was saving hard from her job, with the aim of going to law school. It had been a bitter disappointment on leaving university to have to give up her place. Her mother, in the middle of a divorce from her second husband, suddenly wasn't in a position to pay the fees. Not that Olivia, always a little giddy-headed, could understand her daughter's enthusiasm for the law with its sane, calm logic.

At twenty-four, Alexandra seemed to have her future clearly planned. And then, at a social function she'd attended with her boss, she had met Jim Logan. It had been almost as though there had been some strange jolt of recognition between them, some sense that they were inevitably intended to be linked together. In the space of a few dizzy weeks he had swept her off her feet. For the first time she began to realise what a totally disastrous mixture of cynical caution and romantic idealism she was.

Her cynicism made her wary of marriage, while as a result of her romantic idealism she was still a virgin. If she slept with Jim, she knew that for her it would be a commitment as complete as marriage. At the time it had all been more than she could understand herself, let alone explain to Jim. In a sudden panic about where their relationship was leading, she had started to put up all the barriers she'd used with her previous boyfriends, one of them being her career. Only Jim had been more persistent and, furthermore, with the sexual rapport between them the inevitable happened. The third time he asked her to marry him, they were in bed and he had just seduced her.

A hot tear traced down her cheek and she brushed it away impatiently. She mustn't look back—it only tore at her heart. Neither must she give in to the dark notion that children often repeated the pattern set by their parents. With Roxby, she would prove she was capable of making a lasting marriage.

She turned her head on the pillow and looked mutinously at her ex-husband. The statement he had made to her over dinner had highlighted the one small niggle of doubt she had about her engagement. What he had said about her flashing fire at him was typical of his male conceit, and yet she would feel a little easier if she and Roxby were lovers . . .

Finally she drifted off into fitful sleep. It was the pain in her right shoulder that woke her. She groaned

inwardly and sat up. An unreasonable resentment
stirred against Jim, whose rhythmic breathing hadn't
altered. The night was starting to seem endless.

With sudden decisiveness Alexandra got off the sofa
and crept soundlessly to the far side of the large bed. A
lighter sleeper than he was, she would drop off for a few
blissful hours, be up before him, and he would never
guess she had shared his bed.

With a sigh of contentment she snuggled under the
covers, careful to keep well away from him and, in a few
minutes, was asleep again. When she next came back to
consciousness it was morning. The early light filtered
through the curtains, telling her that the storm was over
and the sun was shining on the Mediterranean. She
stretched languorously. Turning dreamily on her side,
she rolled against Jim. She gave a soundless gasp, her
heart jolting. The haze of sleep vanished. It was more
than time she got up!

Pushing her hands against the mattress, she was
about to slide away from him when he gave a slight
grunt and enveloped her in a hug. She went rigid, her
eyes widening with alarm. She had already coloured at
the intimate contact, but as Jim drew her closer she
blushed still more fiercely. The length of his naked body
was warm and powerful against hers, making her go hot
and shaky. She closed her eyes in despair. Trapped, she
couldn't move for fear of waking him. She could only
hope that in a minute he would turn away, releasing her
enough for her to slither out of bed.

But he showed no sign of doing so at the moment.
Alexandra bit her lip. The strength and warmth of him
was too enticing, reminding her of the countless times
she had slept with his body wrapped behind hers. His
hand moved sensuously on the curve of her waist, and
she drew a shuddering breath, fighting the forbidden

stirring of pleasure. She felt his caressing fingers find the soft swell of her breast and her lips parted, a soft moan escaping her.

And then, without warning, he grabbed savagely hold of her by the wrists, pushing her roughly against the pillows as he leaned over her. She was as shaken as if a sleeping panther had suddenly pounced. Speechless, she stared up into his face, the anger she saw there striking trepidation right through her.

'What the hell do you think you're playing at?' he demanded in a grating undertone.

'Let go of me!' she breathed, trying to sit up.

But Jim was having none of it. He resisted effortlessly her frantic attempts to rise, the weight of his body imprisoning her, his thigh drawn across hers with an intimacy that made her give a choked cry.

'Let go of you?' he said raspingly. 'Are you sure that's what you want? Because you were enjoying yourself plenty a moment ago, weren't you, my frustrated little wife?'

'Get off me,' she said, forcing the words out through clenched teeth. 'I hate you!'

'You mean fantasy time's over?' he jeered, his eyes glinting ominously.

'There . . . there was no fantasy time,' she said, horrified by the sudden catch in her voice. 'You . . . you just grabbed hold of me.'

His hands that held her wrists relaxed a little, puzzled speculation replacing the dangerous glitter in his eyes. The racking moment dragged on, ending with the sound of a light tap at the door. Jim drew a rasping breath.

'I'll be right with you,' he called quite calmly as, lifting his body off Alexandra, he drew her up into a sitting position.

She stared at him mutely, too shaken even to react to

his nudity as he shrugged on his wrap before going to unlock the door to take the breakfast tray from the maid. Then, as he set it down, she slithered off the bed, conscious that she was trembling from head to foot.

Jim flicked a glance at her, a frown appearing between his eyes.

'What did you think I was going to do?' he asked curtly. 'Rape you?'

'It . . . it did cross my mind,' she said tightly, her voice still not under control.

'I didn't realise two years of marriage had left you with such a high opinion of me,' he said in a harsh undertone, dragging a hand through his black hair. His face that had been set hard, as though he was exercising a fierce control over some extreme emotion, softened a little. Quietly he added, 'I'm sorry, Alex. I didn't mean to scare you.'

She nodded and whispered unsteadily, 'I . . . I should have stayed on the sofa.'

He came towards her, surprising her by putting an arm round her with rough tenderness and brushing her forehead with his lips.

'I hope Roxby makes a better shot at understanding you than I did,' he said, the humour in his voice more abrasive than usual. 'Now, stop treating me like an ogre and come and have a cup of coffee.'

Alexandra thought that after what had happened between them she would never be able to be spontaneous with him again. She was wrong. When, having dressed, she joined him on the balcony, he was both patient and teasing with her, until she began to relax with him.

The sun was splashing its golden colours on the sea and the day promised to be gloriously fine.

'You'll have a good trip across to the mainland,' Jim

remarked. 'I've been invited to spend the day on a yacht with a few friends, so I'll drive you down to the harbour.'

It would have been surly to refuse his offer. He was a natural driver and manoeuvred the car he'd hired through the narrow streets with a skill Alexandra grudgingly had to admire. The steamer was already in, and seeing how crowded the harbour was he said, 'It may take me some time to find a space to park, and you don't want to miss the ferry, so I'll drop you here.'

'Fine,' she agreed, adding stiffly, 'And . . . and thanks for your help.'

'My pleasure.'

She got out of the car and then promptly, rashly, made up her mind. Putting a hand on the side of the open door, she leaned forward and said before her bravado could desert her, 'By the way, just for the record—when I married you it wasn't to get through law school.'

She pushed the door shut, turning away quickly. Her heart was thudding, but mostly she was conscious of a fierce satisfaction that she had finally set him right.

CHAPTER FOUR

THE PLANE had been delayed for over an hour on the runway at Naples because of a problem with a fuel valve, but, however late she was landing at Heathrow, Alexandra knew that Roxby would still be waiting to meet her off the flight. It was because he was so reliable that he hadn't joined her as planned. The court case hadn't turned out as he had expected, involving him immediately in launching an appeal.

From the cabin window she watched the twinkling lights of Heathrow grow bigger and bigger as the plane began its final descent. There was a slight jolt as the wheels touched down, and then the engines died to a muted throb as the plane taxied into position. Gathering up her things, Alexandra joined the queue of disembarking passengers.

Although it was getting on for eleven at night, the airport was as busy as ever, but she was channelled efficiently through into the arrivals hall, where she spotted her fiancé almost immediately. He was standing scanning the passengers, and she saw him before he saw her.

Well-built and with wide shoulders, he gave the impression of being taller than he was. His neatly trimmed, dusty blond hair showed the first light frost of silver at the temples, adding to his distinguished looks. The moment he caught sight of her his face broke into his confident smile and he put a hand up and waved.

She quickened her pace, abandoning her luggage trolley as he elbowed his way through the crush to envelop her in a hug.

'Welcome home, darling,' he said, his lips against her cheek.

Alexandra clung to him a minute, conscious of a curious little feeling of relief that his arms felt as comforting as ever.

'I hope you haven't had too long a wait,' she said. 'We were late taking off.'

'It doesn't matter,' he smiled. 'Fortunately the information was given out the moment I arrived, so I had time for a quick meal.'

Alexandra found her spirits were lifting just at being with him again. Her encounter with her ex-husband had unsettled her more than she was prepared to admit. But now, reunited with Roxby, the vague feeling of uncertainty had vanished. His charisma might be different from Jim's, but it was no less appealing, she thought loyally, and, more importantly, he would never let her down.

The roads still carried heavy traffic, though the route was quieter than it would have been in the daytime. As he drove, Roxby brought her up to date with what had been happening at work during her absence. But tonight, still undecided about how to mention her ex-husband and Capri to him, she wasn't the usual interested audience. Giving her a speculative glance, he said, 'I think you're tired.'

'I am a little,' she admitted.

He took a hand off the wheel and patted hers.

'Well, we'll soon have you home. You can have a good lie-in tomorrow, and then I thought you and I would go and look round some houses. While you've been away I've had a few more particulars sent from the estate agents. It's not long now till our wedding. We ought to make a decision soon.'

'Do the particulars sound promising?' she asked.

She wanted to start their married life together somewhere new. It seemed easier that way, although Roxby had said she could have a free hand with altering his bachelor house. His place somehow lacked the homely feel she liked, and it looked so interior-designed that she knew if she moved in with him she would be too tentative to change a thing.

'A couple of them are certainly worth viewing,' said Roxby. 'But to begin with I want us to have another look at the house we went round before you left for Sorrento.'

'It had a good location,' she agreed, 'but the dining-room was a little on the small side.'

'You can't expect to find everything you're looking for in a house,' Roxby chided gently.

'You're right,' she answered. 'I suppose we should take another look at it.'

The trouble was, she thought, as he swung his Rover into her drive, that although she was determined to like the properties they viewed she couldn't help regretting just a little the comfort and convenience of her own home. Fronting on to a triangular-shaped green and with a low gabled roof and small windows, it had a cottage-style prettiness about it.

While Roxby carried her suitcases upstairs, she went into the kitchen where Ellen had left a pint of milk in the fridge. She had the kettle on for coffee when he joined her, and they chatted while she set out the cups. But on her part the conversation was slightly forced. She was trying to find the right opening to mention Jim.

She glanced round as the cat-flap opened and her black and white tom came into the kitchen. About two years old, he still had the touch of the kitten about him, and he ran towards her with a touching little cry of welcome.

'Jingles!' she laughed, scooping him up into her arms. 'It didn't take you long to know I was home, did it?'

'I suppose he heard our voices——' Roxby began, but broke off and sneezed suddenly. Taking out a large white handkerchief, he immediately sneezed again.

'I'm sorry,' Alexandra apologised, 'I forgot about your allergy. Perhaps you'd better go into the sitting-room. I won't be a minute with the coffee.'

Roxby tucked his handkerchief back into his pocket and headed for the door. Pausing there, he joked, 'I think one day you're going to have to choose between me and Jingles. I hesitate to say it, because I know you're fond of the little chap, but I think the answer really is to find him a new home.'

Alexandra set Jingles down on his paws. Ignorant of their conversation, he began to rub round her ankles, purring loudly and making her feel still more of a traitress for contemplating parting with him.

'I expect Ellen would have him for me,' she said, adding, trying to sound less regretful, 'He'll probably prefer that to moving, anyway. Cats get very attached to places.'

'That would be an excellent solution,' said Roxby, quickly settling Jingles' future.

Alexandra joined him in the sitting-room. He waited till she had set the tray down on the coffee-table, and then caught hold of her hand to draw her down on the sofa beside him.

'It's so good to have you back,' he smiled.

She rested her head against his shoulder, liking the feel of his jacket's roughness against her cheek. And then Jim came into her mind again. Promptly she sat forward and handed Roxby his coffee-cup. Every time she thought of Capri, she found it hard to be natural with him. Obviously *he* hadn't sensed anything was different between them, but *she* was conscious of it, and for that reason alone she must tell him. She didn't have to give him a long, serious explanation, just a carefully casual account of how she had been stranded would be enough to make her relax and to rekindle the usual rapport between them.

The trouble was that Roxby wasn't giving her much of a chance to get an opening. They had talked about a number of things before he finally said, 'Well, how was Sorrento? I hope it didn't spoil it for you too much that I was unable to be with you.'

'It wasn't quite the same,' she admitted, bracing herself for what was to follow. 'And apart from that I was sorry the case went against you. Also——'

'These things happen,' Roxby cut across her. 'Luckily, with us both being in the same line, you understand. I count myself very fortunate, you know, to be marrying such a reasonable, sweet-natured woman.'

'Thank you,' she said faintly.

Why did he have to interrupt? Alexandra was getting a little tired of the suspense of waiting poised to begin.

'So what did you think of Pompeii?'

'Actually I . . . I wanted to tell you about Capri.'

He threw up a protesting hand and laughed.

'Spare me! I can imagine—everywhere crowded out and the whole island horribly commercialised. Well, I did warn you. I suppose you wished you hadn't made the trip.'

She drew breath for a reply and then, in despair, gave up. Why was she making life unnecessarily difficult for herself? After all, the whole episode had been completely innocent. Maybe she was getting it all out of proportion. She believed in honesty in a relationship, but wasn't she running the risk of making Roxby jealous and suspicious?

'Yes, afterwards I did wish I'd stayed on the mainland,' she agreed drily.

'Tell you what,' he said, taking her hand. 'As soon as I get this appeal sorted out we'll take a short break away together—somewhere romantic. Paris, perhaps.'

Roxby stayed a short while longer and then, commenting on how late it was, stood up to leave. As usual, he kissed her goodnight very tenderly. Alexandra stayed in the doorway, silhouetted by the hall light, to wave as his car turned at the corner, not quite as carefree as she seemed. The physical side of their relationship had been vaguely on her mind ever since Jim's infuriating comment.

Right from the beginning her fiancé had treated her with perfect gentlemanliness, so much so that on the one occasion when he'd become more passionate she'd been taken so by surprise he had thought he'd shocked her and had immediately apologised. He'd jumped to the conclusion that she wanted their relationship properly sanctified before they slept together and, always reticent about expressing her feelings, she had somehow found it impossible to correct him by telling him her moral code wasn't quite as strict as that.

Tonight, though, she was almost relieved that she had her supposed scruples to shelter behind. Seeing Jim again had reminded her too evocatively of the feverish response she was capable of giving to a man. She needed the memory of that to dim a little, or else she'd start giving way to doubts.

A sound night's sleep and the quiet of an early Sunday morning helped to restore her sense of tranquillity. She hadn't been up long when Ellen called round to see her. Her grandmother was a practical, resourceful woman, and Alexandra loved her dearly. During her childhood she had spent a considerable amount of time with her. Whenever her mother's love-life had been particularly traumatic she'd found herself packed off to Dursley. She was always sorry when the periods of calm came to an end.

Then, as now, Ellen was her closest confidante. But not even she knew about Jim's infidelity. It wasn't just that his betrayal had knocked her pride so badly, destroying her trust in him and hurting her confidence as a woman. It also had something to do with a strange reluctance to tarnish him in Ellen's eyes.

Rather than admit the truth, she had said they were splitting up because they just weren't suited, trying to hide how she felt by acting in a sane, reasonable manner, although at the time she'd been an unexploded bomb of anger and pain. How successful she had been she wasn't sure. Ellen, though she never pried, could be very discerning.

She unwrapped the cameo brooch Alexandra had bought in Sorrento for her with an exclamation of surprise and delight.

'Oh, how lovely!' She fastened it quickly at the throat of her silk blouse, and Alexandra saw how right her choice had been. Ellen, with her white hair swept into an elegant french pleat, always conveyed an impression of serenity.

'Wasn't it a coincidence, your running into Jim in Sorrento?' she remarked.

'You . . . you know about that?' Alexandra faltered.

'Yes, he called round the day before yesterday and mentioned that you'd bumped into each other in the hotel. As you were on your own, I expect you were quite pleased to see him.'

'I wouldn't go as far as to say that,' Alexandra said darkly.

'Oh, come now! You divorced amicably and Jim's good company. He knows not to take himself too seriously, and he knows the secret of enjoying life.'

'He's a playboy.'

'Nonsense!' Ellen said reprovingly. 'There's nothing of the playboy about Jim. Do you know, you can sound as irrational as Olivia at times?'

'I hope not,' laughed Alexandra. 'I have no intention of leading the sort of life Mother's had. What I want is to be steady, responsible and settled.'

Ellen nodded, a thoughtful look in her eyes before she recalled herself and said, 'By the way, I hope you didn't mind my telling Jim about your wedding plans.'

'Why should I mind?'

'You must admit,' Ellen said carefully, 'you can be a little bit prickly where he's concerned.'

'Well, I don't mean to be. Though I think he had a downright nerve the way he . . .' Alexandra broke off, remembering all too vividly the insolent way Jim had kissed her. Hurriedly she changed what she'd been going to say to, '. . . the way he kept quizzing me about my plans.'

'I'm sure he was only making conversation. After all, *I'd* already put him in the picture about Roxby.'

Ellen made it sound as though she'd brought Jim up to date with an unfortunate mishap. It made Alexandra wonder just what impression Ellen had conveyed of her fiancé. She said suspiciously, 'I hope you and Jim didn't spend the whole time discussing me.'

'Now you are being prickly! No, we talked about his new house.'

'His new house?' she echoed.

'Didn't he tell you? He's just sold his flat in St John's

Wood, and has moved out to a four-bedroomed
detached in Rickmansworth.'

'What does he want a house that size for?' Alexandra
asked promptly, irked that when Jim had played the
inquisitor so skilfully with her he should have been so
close about his own affairs.

'Property's a good investment, and I suppose he's
thinking of marrying again. Attractive and successful
men of thirty-four don't stay unattached for long, and
the two of you have been divorced for almost three
years.'

'I can't imagine Jim throwing in his lot with marriage
again,' said Alexandra, trying to quell the riotous
indignation the very idea of Jim remarrying evoked.
'He'd find it too restricting. He's far more likely to live
with a woman for a couple of years and then go on to
someone new.'

Ellen stroked Jingles under the chin and, with a
slight, eloquent shrug, discounted what Alexandra had
just said. With a sickening jolt Alexandra realised that
perhaps Jim really was planning to start again with a
new wife. The news was all the more unexpected
because she'd assumed he still regretted his break-up
with Juliette. Unless they'd since got things together!

A riotous fury went through her at the thought. Was
Jim engaged to Juliette? Her eyes went dark and stormy
as she stubbornly refused to ask outright how much
Ellen knew. Yet she couldn't stand not knowing. It took
every ounce of her self-control to keep her voice even
and casual as she said,

'Did Jim say he was thinking of getting married?'

'Alexandra, are you fishing?' asked Ellen, amused.

'No!' she snapped, and then, feeling herself colour,
she added defensively, 'Well, why shouldn't I take an
interest in him? I was married to him for two years.'

She broke off, remembering to her chagrin that she had used exactly the same explanation for prying into Jim's life as he had used that night on Capri for cross-examining her about hers.

'Perhaps if you hadn't been so career-minded, you and Jim might still be together,' Ellen commented.

'That had nothing to do with Jim and me splitting up.'

'Your career certainly didn't help things,' Ellen said gently. 'And I think you know it.' She saw the sharp lights of pain that had come into her granddaughter's expressive blue eyes and went on, 'I'm not blaming you. It was only natural that you wanted to take your solicitor's exams, having got your law degree. I only wish *I'd* had the money to pay for you to go to law school. Then you'd have already been qualified when you met Jim, and you wouldn't have spent all your time studying instead of working at your marriage.'

'My mistake was getting involved with Jim in the first place,' Alexandra answered. 'And I certainly shouldn't have got involved so quickly. If I'd known him longer, I might have judged his character a little better.'

'There's nothing wrong with Jim's character. Though I do think he should have kept you on a slightly tighter rein.'

'Gran!' she exclaimed indignantly. 'What a thing to say!'

'I mean it. The trouble was that although Jim was only a few years older than you he was much more mature. I think he sensed you were afraid of the commitment of marriage, and because of it he tried never to restrict you. And it's not many men who'd be big enough to do that.'

'That's utter nonsense!' Alexandra said stormily, thinking of Jim's betrayal. The conversation was already much too painful, threatening to bring to the surface emotions she kept buried deep. Wanting to change the subject, she went on briskly, 'In any case, what happened between Jim and me is in the past. All I'm interested in now is the future.'

'Well, you know what they say about advice,' sighed Ellen. 'Don't give it. And perhaps Roxby will turn out to have hidden depths.'

'There's nothing wrong with Roxby the way he is. Listen, I put my heart before my head once and where did it get me? You'd think I'd have had more sense. I work as a solicitor. I'm good at coming up with the rational solution, but did I apply that kind of reasoning to my private life? No, I had to go and marry Jim. Well, I'm not being swept off my feet again. I've learned to look long and hard at a relationship, and with Roxby I like what I see. The two of us couldn't be better suited if we'd been matched up by a computer. I don't want to go through life alone . . .'

'Although you're quite prepared to go through it childless,' Ellen interrupted disapprovingly.

Thrown from her line of argument, Alexandra took a minute to answer, 'There's nothing wrong with not wanting children.'

'I thought you wanted them rather badly at one time.'

'Yes, I know I did,' Alexandra sighed. 'I just wanted to qualify first and, looking back, it's no bad thing I didn't have any. If Jim and I had had a baby——'

'You wouldn't have broken up,' Ellen cut across her again.

'It would have made no difference,' Alexandra disagreed soberly. 'But *if* I'd had a child I'd have wanted it to have a good, stable upbringing, not the sort of home life I had. I'd rather not have children than put them through the trauma of divorce.'

'Admittedly your childhood was very unsettled,' Ellen conceded. 'But you and I had some fine times together.'

'Yes, I know we did,' Alexandra said warmly. 'But just the same I wouldn't want my child brought up partly by its grandmother because its parents keep arguing. And I certainly wouldn't want it to have a father that walks out flat.'

'Jim would never have done that.'

'Maybe, but he can't touch Roxby when it comes to reliability. And that's what I'm looking for this time.'

'Well, certainly Roxby is predictable,' Ellen murmured ambiguously. Seeing the estate agent's leaflets he had left for Alexandra to look through, she asked, changing the subject, 'Have you got more house-hunting planned for today?'

'Yes, I'm expecting Roxby any time now. We thought we'd have a pub lunch in one of the Chiltern villages and then we're going over a couple.'

'In which case, dear, I won't keep you talking.'

It wasn't until she had gone and Alexandra was in the kitchen that she realised that in being sidetracked she hadn't got an answer from Ellen as to whether Jim was about to be married. She faintly suspected her grandmother of deliberately withholding the information. Alexandra had no intention of making it look as if she cared one way or another by asking again. Besides, a four-bedroomed house in Rickmansworth was almost answer enough.

But it didn't tell her who his fiancée was. Increasingly she suspected Juliette. She turned the coffee-cups out on to the draining-board with such vigorous speed, she hit one of the handles against the tap and for a minute thought she'd broken it. She must try to bring stillness to the fury inside her, and yet she could not. Even after three years, Jim's involvement was a knife-thrust of anger and pain. Damn him! she thought savagely. He was nothing to her now, so why should she care that he was finally marrying his mistress?

The friendly ambience of the sixteenth-century pub where she and Roxby had lunch helped her unwind a little, and she was quite taken with one of the houses they looked over. As they came away Roxby said, after they had discussed its merits, 'The owners are keen to sell, so quite possibly we could get a bit of a bargain. I suggest I put in a low offer first thing tomorrow and we set the ball rolling.'

She agreed, and with that decision made she started to feel slightly more cheerful again. The fact that she could take positive steps about the future proved how completely she was over her first husband.

It was the following Tuesday that she noticed Jim's white BMW parked outside Ellen's. He'd obviously meant what he'd said about helping her grandmother get the garden into better shape. Hearing the whine of a chainsaw, Alexandra went to the french windows. Without meaning to, she stood there watching as he worked, lopping the branches of the massive blue cedar which overhung the guttering. Versatile, he seemed to be able to turn his hand to anything, and he looked every bit as attractive in jeans and a check shirt as he had in a black dinner-jacket on Capri.

The evening sunlight was lovely, but his presence next door kept her as a virtual prisoner in the house. She had no wish to be forced to speak to him. In fact, she hoped it would be a long time before she encountered him again.

She was over-optimistic. On Saturday when she went next door, it was to be greeted by Ellen, who was wearing a fluted navy-blue skirt with a cream jacquard blouse.

'I'm so glad you've called, dear,' she began in a flurry. 'I can't seem to do up my pearls.'

'I hadn't realised you were going out or I'd have looked in sooner,' said Alexandra, following her into the drawing-room. 'You haven't forgotten we've been invited over to Mother's this evening?'

'I'll be back before then,' Ellen said brightly. She handed Alexandra the string of pearls. 'Jim's taking me to a matinée performance of *High Society*.'

'Jim?' Alexandra began in surprise, looking up from fastening the pearls.

'Yes. I haven't been to the theatre in such a while,' said Ellen, breaking off as the doorbell went and exclaiming, 'That will be Jim now. Would you run and let him in?'

Alexandra, whose pulse had quickened quite irrationally, stood for a moment as if rooted to the spot. She felt as if she'd unwittingly walked into an ambush. She shook the ridiculous notion off. Afraid that she was behaving altogether too transparently, she went briskly into the hall.

Without meaning to, she flashed a glance in the mirror as she passed. It was too late now to wish she hadn't spent the morning pottering in the house in comfy baggy slacks and a cotton top. Taking a steadying breath, she opened the door.

Jim's height forced her to adjust her gaze upwards.

'Ellen's expecting you,' she began, using an excess of distant politeness in an attempt to appear composed. 'Won't you come in?'

His dark eyes mocked her.

'I hope you're not acting the ice-maiden on my account,' he said with satiric gravity. 'I'd hate to think our night together on Capri had upset you.'

Alexandra mastered the impulse to flash back with a quick answer. Instead she stared back at him, despite the little blush that had crept into her cheeks. The knowledge that he was engaged made her all the more determined to put him down. Coolly she said, 'As it so happens, I've forgotten about that night. And where you're concerned, Jim, the chilliness is *not* an act.'

'Do you want me to prove you wrong?' he asked softly.

An uneasy prickling ran along her skin. She must stop issuing him with needless challenges. Aware of the static between them, she thought better of a retaliatory answer. She dragged her gaze away from his and went ahead of him into the drawing-room with the quixotic notion that she was fleeing to sanctuary.

'Now, where did I leave my jacket?' Ellen fluttered as Jim came in. She swept him an apologetic smile. 'It must be upstairs. I won't be a minute.'

'I'll run up and get it for you,' Alexandra volunteered hastily.

'Now then, you don't have to treat me as an old lady yet,' Ellen said humorously. 'You stay and keep Jim company.'

She went out of the room, and Alexandra, trying desperately to appear at ease, took a seat in one of the armchairs. Jim strolled over to the sofa. In a grey suit and white shirt he looked disturbingly and blatantly male.

She hunted for something to say, wanting to destroy the charged tension that always seemed present between them. Jim broke the silence for her. Looking her over in leisurely appraisal, he drawled, 'If I'd known you were going to be at a loose end this afternoon, I'd have got a third ticket.'

'I'm not at a loose end,' she corrected him, nettled,

'though I have to say I would have thought *you'd* have had plans other than the theatre for this afternoon.'

'I take it there's some cryptic meaning behind that comment,' Jim said drily.

'Yes, there is,' she said coldly. 'In view of the fact that you're getting married shortly I expected you to be with your fiancée.'

Jim's eyes narrowed on her face.

'Who told you I was getting married again?'

'Ellen,' she supplied shortly.

'Well, I never!' he commented, amused. 'What a perceptive woman your grandmother is.'

'Don't keep me in the dark,' Alexandra said, sarcasm disguising the venomous anger she felt. 'Who's the lucky lady?'

'With your clear lawyer-like mind, why don't you try puzzling it out?' he mocked.

She got swiftly to her feet.

'I don't even have to. I can guess, knowing your taste for tarty women!'

With sudden predatory speed Jim also stood up, taking hold of her by the arm.

'Let go of me!' she demanded furiously. 'And if you think you're going to bully me into retracting what I've just said, you're damn well wrong. Juliette Stanton will always be, in my opinion, a first-class bitch and a first-class tart!'

She heard Ellen's tread on the stairs, and with a start snatched her arm away from him. Jim's grip had been so firm, the wrench bruised her, but in her hot anger she scarcely cared.

'There,' Ellen announced blithely as she came into the room, 'I'm ready at last!'

Alexandra, her heart still thudding unevenly, couldn't rise immediately to small talk. She missed the keen, narrowed glance Jim slanted her, but she was so conscious of the turbulent, charged atmosphere between them, it seemed staggering that Ellen was unaware of it.

'Well then, shall we go?' asked Jim, offering her grandmother his arm.

Patting her chignon, Alexandra saw them to the door. If Jim could act as if they hadn't been interrupted in the middle of a fight, so could she.

'Enjoy the show,' she said.

'I'm sure we will,' Ellen smiled. 'It's got such a lively score. I enjoyed the film of it so much.'

She went ahead of Jim down the path. He turned to Alexandra, putting a finger to his lips and then grazing her cheek with it before she could dodge away.

'I'll catch up with you later, Alex.'

He smiled cynically as he saw the flash of temper in her blue eyes at his insolent caress. She couldn't even resort to slamming the door shut in protest, because she too was on her way out.

She stared coldly at him as he walked off, her hatred of him fuelled still further by the physical grace of his pantherish stride. There was almost something of a threat in his parting comment to her, and with sudden comprehension she realised she had not had her last clash with her ex-husband.

CHAPTER FIVE

ALEXANDRA'S look was still charged with animosity as Jim opened the passenger door for Ellen, who turned to give her a little wave. Recollecting herself hastily, Alexandra smiled, and with a friendly wave back she crossed the drive to her own front door with the infuriating comprehension that Jim was amused by her frustration at her inability to get the better of him.

Inside, the piece of acting over, her eyes reverted to a stormy blue again. She tried to take herself in check, determined not to allow Jim to get under her skin in this way. The fact that Juliette was his type of woman only showed how right she was to have chosen reliable Roxby as her future husband.

To chase Jim from her thoughts, she started some housework. But as therapy it wasn't effective. She wandered into the garden and sat down absently on the sunwarmed steps that led down from the patio on to the lawn. She didn't want to remember the early days of her marriage to Jim, and yet, as her anger faded, a wistfulness caught hold of her that she couldn't seem to shake off. Not wanting to identify the reason for it, she stood up and went back indoors.

The sun had faded by the time she'd finished her chores. Feeling hot and untidy, she washed her hair and then took a long, relaxing bath. She had just stepped out of it and was pulling on her short towelling robe when the doorbell rang. Tying the belt, she went downstairs and called out tentatively, 'Who is it?'

'Well, it's not Young Lochinvar!'

Immediately Alexandra pulled the lapels of her robe more closely together, recognising both Jim's well-pitched voice and his brand of humour. He *would* find amusing the reference to Lochinvar, who had rescued his bride as she had been about to be handed to another, she thought crossly.

What on earth did he want? In fighting spirit, she decided it would give her a great deal of satisfaction to order him off her property. Boldly she opened the front door and, as she did so, the telephone started ringing.

Jim's masculine eyes slipped over her, reminding her that not one line of her hidden body was unknown to him. The combination of his raking gaze and the telephone ringing insistently seemed to make her temporarily incapable of dealing with either of them.

'I'll wait while you answer that,' Jim said considerately as he strolled inside.

Alexandra snatched up the receiver, her eyes following him angrily as he disappeared into her sitting-room.

'Ms Challoner?'

Running a hand through her hair, she tried to place the friendly voice. It took her a minute to recognise the informal sales technique and to cut into the preamble by saying curtly that no, she did not want double glazing.

She rang off and, summoning up her self-possession, walked into the sitting-room, where Jim was prowling about.

A bowl of wallflowers and tulips stood on the coffee-table which was placed in the centre of the arrangement of chintz-covered armchairs. A sofa faced the claygate fireplace which gleamed with brass fire-irons.

'I like the way you've done this up,' he commented.

Alexandra couldn't help but be conscious of a flicker of pleasure at his compliment, even if it was mingled with a certain annoyance. The way Jim was examining the room, he might have been planning on moving in.

'It has a nice restful feel,' he went on, 'but then you always did have a flair when it came to decorating a place.'

Idly he picked up her Tolkien novel and glanced at it. She felt a prickle of annoyance at his interest in what she was reading. It was high time he remembered he was an intruder in her house, not someone who had a right to be here. Advancing towards him, she took the book out of his hands.

A warning glitter came into his eyes, but his voice was even as he said, 'I've just dropped Ellen off.'

Alexandra retreated a prudent distance from him. Going to stand by the open door, she enquired with cool sarcasm, 'Did you call especially to tell me that?'

'No, I called especially to get you out of the bath,' he answered derisively, before mocking, 'You know, this has overtones of Italy. Almost every time I've seen you lately, you seem to be stripped off.'

'Through no fault of my own. Now, what do you want?'

Jim's eyes travelled over her, and he seemed for an instant to debate his answer. She felt her heart lurch at his threatening attractiveness and, maddened that he could have this effect on her, she snapped, 'I've told you before not to look at me like that!'

'What's eating you? The fact that looking is as much as I'm doing?'

'You have the cheapest line of repartee I've ever heard!' she flashed back. 'I suppose it's the company you mix with. Well, may I suggest you keep your innuendoes for your fiancée. She's brazen enough to appreciate them.'

'My engagement to Juliette's really got you going,

hasn't it?' he jeered. 'What is it, Alex, a touch of jealousy?'

'How typical of your conceit!' she exclaimed. 'Far from being jealous, I wish you joy of each other. I'd say you were both excellently matched.'

She knew from the glitter in his eyes that her ringing sarcasm was pushing him too far. A prickling awareness of danger ran over her skin, and in an alarmed attempt to reduce the forcefield of static between them she put frost in her voice as she went on, 'Now tell me why you're here, and then get out.'

With a flutter of fear, she wondered if she'd already gone too far. She was starting to heed that hard look in Jim's face. Fortunately for her, his forbearance had the upper hand.

'I called to give you a message from Ellen,' he told her levelly. 'She says she's sorry, but she's going to have to cancel dinner this evening, so she won't be troubling you and Roxby for a lift.'

'She's not feeling ill, is she?' asked Alexandra, concerned, as Jingles came into the room.

'No, she's just feeling a bit tired after the theatre, and your mother's dinner parties can be rather exhausting.'

Tacitly she shared his opinion, but that didn't make her modify the cool glare she gave him. Jim, who had bent down to scoop Jingles up into his large man's hand, missed it.

'When did you get your cat?' he asked.

'I didn't,' she answered. 'He moved in with me around Christmas time.'

'He's a nice little fellow,' he remarked as he scratched the cat under his chin. 'What do you call him?'

'Jingles. He came at Christmas. "Jingle Bells"—you know the song. Hence Jingles.'

Jim laughed at her explanation, and she realised with

a start of annoyance as she caught herself smiling that his charismatic personality was lulling her into an illusory sense of rapport with him. Determined to break the mood, she said, meaning for him to take his cue to leave, 'Well, thank you for the message.'

Instead he came towards her.

'Isn't that the bathrobe I gave you?' he asked.

'Possibly . . . yes . . . I believe it is,' she said, rather breathlessly. Crossing her hands protectively to hug her arms, she went on in a rush, 'Jim, I'm getting cold. I'd like to put some clothes on.'

She did not like the sudden uneasiness she felt. With a distance between them, and strengthened by anger, she could fight Jim with spirit. When he was close to her like this, her defences seemed as shaky as a house of cards.

'If you're cold, I could suggest a way of warming you up,' he taunted, resting a casual hand on the door-frame so it was almost level with his head.

His virile masculinity seemed to be enveloping her. The faint scent of his aftershave was as evocative as a half-forgotten song. She found that her heart was beating like a hammer, and with a mixture of anger and anguish that he could make her react like this she said with a surge of hostility, 'Jim, leave me alone.'

Instead of complying, he bent and brushed her temple with his lips.

'Do you know your hair smells of freesias?'

She swung her hand up, only to have him snatch hold of her wrist before her palm could connect with his cheek.

'I said leave me alone!' she snapped, praying that he wouldn't sense the tremulous weakness that had engulfed her.

'You're turning into quite the little spitfire,' he jeered

softly. 'It makes me wonder what you'd do if I kissed
you.'

'Stop it . . .' she breathed angrily, pushing her free
hand against his shoulder in a panic. 'If you so much as
dare . . .'

Her protest was silenced as Jim bent his head, his
mouth finding hers. A sensuous tremor ran up her
spine, making the fleeting notion she'd had of staying
passive in his arms vanish along with every other
coherent thought. For a moment she struggled, but his
powerful arms only wrapped her more tightly against
his lean hardness.

The firmness of his lips as they parted hers made her
go hot and shaky. She'd half forgotten what it was like
to be kissed like this, with a plundering sensual
enjoyment that set her slim body suddenly on fire with
longing. Reality was lost in the urgent storm of desire.
Tangling her fingers in the crisp, dark hair at the nape
of his neck, she gave a soft moan, daggers of pleasure
shooting through her as Jim brought the slight arc of
her into a still tighter fit against him.

He kissed her long and deeply, and when finally he
raised his head she felt dizzy and reckless. Still caught in
the mad enchantment of the moment, she closed her
eyes, arching her throat as he pressed ardent kisses
down to the sensitive pulse at its base.

'You witch,' he muttered raggedly.

Combing his fingers into her hair, he looked down at
her, hunger flaring in his eyes as they interlocked with
hers. Alexandra breathed his name shakily, tongues of
fire licking through her veins as he parted her robe. His
hand slid inside, caressing her bare skin, while his
mouth found hers again. The pleasure of his touch was
igniting her to delirium. Feverishly she pushed his jacket
from his shoulders, obsessed with the need to feel him

throughout every inch of her. His palms roamed over the smoothness of her back, and she moaned again softly, the ringing that sounded faintly in her head drowned by the mutual swell of passion. The calm, sane double chime came again, and suddenly the enchantment was shattered into a myriad pieces.

At the same moment Jim raised his head and growled, 'If that's the front door, forget you're home.'

She turned her head away from the kiss. The doorbell was breaking into what her conscience should never have allowed in the first place.

'Let go of me,' she commanded shakily, utterly shocked by the force of her desire.

His jaw tightened. He tilted her chin back towards him, and for an instant they stared into each other's eyes.

'I want to answer it,' she insisted mutinously, pushing against his shoulders, and relieved when he let her go free.

She stumbled into the hall. Sashing the belt of her robe, she reached the door, chilly with dismay at what had been interrupted, and furious with herself for her lack of self-control. The moment she had got rid of whoever was at the front door, she was going to have the most blazing set-to with her ex-husband. She opened it and then stood there, horror-struck, as she saw Roxby.

He couldn't be real! Alexandra slid her back against the door-frame because without some kind of support she wasn't sure she wouldn't slither to the floor.

'Roxby——' she began weakly, knowing she was blushing right down to the neckline of her robe.

'I do apologise for calling at an inopportune moment.'

Inopportune? He just didn't know! She realised he

thought he'd thrown her into a confusion of embarrassed modesty, and felt so utterly despicable she could have wept.

'I only stopped by,' he went on, 'to say that I called in at the office this afternoon. The traffic's been dreadful coming out of London, so I may be a little later in picking you up this evening than I'd said.'

She nodded, swallowed and said, 'It . . . it was very thoughtful of you to tell me.'

'Well, I won't keep you at the door, my precious love —it's most unwise to get cold after a bath. See you anon.'

Despite his romantic nature, the most he'd ever called her before was darling or sweetheart. She could only suppose this new endearment was prompted by a sense of masculine protectiveness at having made her blush so fiercely. Aware that Jim must be able to hear every word of their conversation, she wished it could all be a nightmare and she would wake up to find none of it had happened.

''Bye . . . darling,' she said in a cramped voice.

Roxby went off down the path and swiftly Alexandra shut the door behind him, her heart pounding. Suppose he'd asked to come in . . . Suppose for some reason he'd decided to call early and had said he'd wait for her while she dressed? Stung with shame at her behaviour, she stormed back into the sitting-room to confront the man who had made her act so despicably.

'Don't tell me,' Jim began drily. 'That was the fiancé. I must say he gets ten out of ten for timing!'

'Not one word!' she raged. 'You just get out of here—now, this minute!'

'I don't think your fiancé's car has pulled away yet, but if that's what you want . . .'

He started towards the door and she caught hold of his arm, her eyes wide with alarm.

'No!' she protested. 'You can't leave till he's gone.'

Jim smiled knowingly and, to her fury, she realised he was amused by the situation. It was abundantly plain that he had only kissed her in the first place for the male satisfaction of proving he could still make her respond to him. Tremulous from reaction, she exploded, 'I hate you for this! You despicable womaniser! You come into my house, harass me sexually . . .'

'Don't give me that,' he cut across her with a force that stopped her short. 'With those sexy little purring noises you were making, you were loving every minute of it!'

'Yes, all right, for a few minutes I lost my head,' she said stormily. 'But considering how practised you are at seduction, that's not altogether surprising. But let me tell you this. The fact that you were once my husband does not give you any rights over me now. And more than that, I am not going to fail with a second relationship. Damn you, don't you realise you almost put my whole future in jeopardy? Now get out of my house, and out of my life!'

'So you can go back to being the unimpassioned woman?' he jeered lightly.

'I ought to slap your face for that!'

'You can try it if it'll make you feel any better.'

Alexandra glared at him, hearing the warning in his voice. A chasm of danger had opened up in front of her. To lose her self-control with the atmosphere crackling with sexual antagonism would be to invite catastrophe. It was safer to back down, however much it went against the grain. Clenching her fists, she said coldly, 'I will not have you make me into an adulteress!'

A glint of amusement came back into Jim's dark eyes.

'Technically,' he commented mockingly, 'I think you have to be married for that. But you're the lawyer.'

'How typical! I should have guessed you'd find this a joke. After all, what's a bit of adultery as far as you're concerned? *You* can shrug this sort of thing off, but I haven't had the practice you have and I can't. This isn't the way I behave. Do you understand?'

'Not even with Roxby?' he jeered.

Temper flashed in her blue eyes. Jim took hold of her by the forearms and pulled her to his shirt. His fingers gripped her with a steely force, and she had the feeling that despite his mocking gaze he would have liked to have shaken her.

'You know,' he went on, 'somehow I can't imagine you turning on for Roxby the way you did with me just now.'

'That's what this was all about, wasn't it?' she flashed back. 'You didn't want me three years ago, but you can't bear to think anyone else might. Well, Roxby does want me, and yes, I do turn on for him!'

A strand of hair fell across her face, and she tossed her head to throw it back, her breasts rising and falling with her angry breathing. As her stormy eyes warred with his, the air seemed to vibrate with menace. Jim's fingers tightened cruelly on her arms, and she almost held her breath in the sudden fear that the tension between them would ignite.

He released her abruptly, the set of his jaw showing that he was keeping his temper in check with great difficulty.

'I think I'd better leave,' he said curtly. 'The sight of you with your hair tumbled and with no clothes on brings out the devil in me.'

'Yes, and stay away from me in future,' she snapped.

'I'll do my best—my precious love.'

Unprepared as she was for his parting shot, the derisive jeer in his voice stung even more. She was too angry to begin to splutter an incoherent reply. In any case, with his pantherish stride Jim was already gone from the room. Snatching up her book, she raced after him into the hall. The self-controlled woman who always thought before she acted had in the last half-hour turned into an impulsive fury.

She hurled the paperback at him, but she wasn't quick enough. It crashed against the oak lintel as the door closed after him, and then fell spine uppermost on to the mat.

But at least the violent gesture helped to relieve her feelings a little. She went back into the sitting-room and sank down wearily on to the sofa, tucking her legs up tightly to her. She could scarcely believe the events of the afternoon. A quiver of unexpected desire went through her, making her eyes grow hot and angry again.

Why did Jim have to remind her of sexual yearnings she'd all but forgotten? Emotionally exhausted, she felt defeated to the point that she was almost resigned to the way his presence in her life seemed to be undermining her relationship with her fiancé.

As though he sensed her distress, Jingles jumped up on the sofa, resting his two front paws on her thigh in mute protest against her sloping lap. Obligingly Alexandra untucked her feet and the little cat started to purr, clawing contentedly at her robe before settling down.

'Jingles, I'm a fool,' she whispered feelingly as she stroked his soft fur. 'I tried being married to the bastard once and it didn't work. He's a womaniser and a liar and I know it, and he hasn't changed one bit . . .'

She didn't want to start replaying the break-up of her marriage, and yet she couldn't seem to stop herself. Deep down she knew she was partly to blame for the gulf that had weakened their relationship.

She'd been determined to make a success of her career. At first Jim had been immensely understanding, and six months after they were married she had begun to study at law school. She'd never expected that, having been out at work, she would find it so hard to go back to being a student. Or perhaps it was because she was so happy with Jim that she didn't study as seriously as she should . . .

It was only as the final exams at the end of the year approached that she realised how far she had got behind. Jim had given her the chance she had always wanted by supporting her at law school, and if she didn't pass she'd show she hadn't merited his faith in her. In a fever of apprehension, she tried to make up the lost time.

Sitting surrounded by law books, she started as Jim put a hand on her shoulder and bent to kiss her.

'Sweetheart, it's almost midnight. Come on, give it a rest. Come to bed.''

Alexandra dragged a harassed hand through her hair.

'I can't—not yet. I've got all this work to do and I can't remember any of these cases. At this rate, I'm going to fail.'

He sat down on the sofa beside her and took hold of her hand.

'OK, so you may have to resit. It won't be the end of the world.'

'Resit?' It was as if he had made a prediction. 'No, I'm not going to resit. I'm going to pass, even if I have to slave every night in order to do it. You paid for me to go to law school . . .'

'Look, damn the fees,' Jim cut across her with sudden wrath. 'They're not important, and neither are these exams. You don't *need* to pass them. You're making life hard for both of us. Do you realise that I hardly get to see you most evenings?'

'Stop pressurising me!' she snapped tautly. 'You don't understand what these exams mean to me. I've got to prove I can do it.'

'I understand they're screwing up our marriage,' he said harshly.

He stood up and strode angrily from the room. Despairingly Alexandra hurled her notes on to the floor and burst into overwrought tears.

It was their first row, but, although the cause of their disagreement remained, it wasn't repeated. Jim didn't tell her again that she should ease up. She knew she was being hard to live with, yet she couldn't give up on what she'd set out to achieve. Neither, without becoming over-emotional, could she seem to explain to Jim how terrified she was of failure, of losing the dream she'd always had of becoming a solicitor, and so being diminished in his eyes.

Gradually a barrier of things unsaid began to grow. Often she was so tired when the day finished she went to sleep immediately, but even when she wasn't tired Jim didn't seem to need her as he had done once in bed. It had hurt her to think that after his initial delight in her his excitement had faded.

But it had never crossed her mind to suspect that he had another woman. She had been naïve in that, because she'd sensed that his secretary was strongly attracted to him. She had thought that Juliette, involved in a long-term relationship with her boyfriend, represented no threat to her, yet just the same she'd been jealous enough to tease Jim about it in a lightly barbed way.

They seemed increasingly to be two polite strangers living separate lives but sharing the same house. Alexandra didn't know what to do to put things right between them. Finally, desperately wanting him to disagree with her, she suggested they try a short separation.

Jim agreed. She drove off to the centre where a revision course was being held that weekend, enveloped in misery. She didn't want a separation. What she'd wanted was for him to insist they sort their problems out. She sat through the first lecture, the words drifting over her. In sudden comprehension she realised the course wasn't worth a thing compared to her marriage. What on earth was she trying to do by proving something to herself? She didn't need to be a shining success so long as Jim still loved her.

The lecture still in progress, she left the room. It was getting late and the roads were empty. Having made her decision, she was impatient to be home. Her heart was hushed with happiness. Everything was going to be all right.

She parked her car in the drive, surprised by the throb of heavy music that was coming from the house. She let herself in. The music drowned her voice as she called out cheerfully to Jim. She was about to go into the lounge, when she froze in the doorway, her eyes widening with shock. The blare of the music was so deafening, he had not heard her come in. He was standing by the stereo and with her arms around his neck was Juliette. She was completely naked.

With a choked gasp Alexandra sagged against the doorframe. Pressing her hand to her mouth, she ran out of the house. The pain that stabbed at her heart was so acute, she felt she couldn't stand it.

She jumped into her car, jammed the gears into first and pulled away. She couldn't credit what a fool she had been. Small wonder Jim no longer wanted her in bed! The uprise of pain was so sharp that suddenly she couldn't stop the sobs. She drove for a while longer, heedless of the tears that ran hotly down her face. Then, pulling over to the side of the road and in the cover of darkness, she rested her arms on the steering-wheel and, bowing her head, she wept bitterly and without hope.

The only place to go was back to the study centre. She spent the rest of the weekend there desperately trying to work out what she should do. She decided it would be useless to confront Jim over the affair. Their marriage was obviously over. She had too much pride to beg him to give Juliette up and, in any case, she was sure it was useless. She would never let him know she had come home unexpectedly that evening. All she could do was to end their marriage with as much quiet dignity as possible.

On Monday when she returned home she told Jim, trying to keep emotion out of her voice, that, having thought it over, a separation wasn't the answer. She wanted a divorce. Grim-faced, he had said he wouldn't fight it.

Jingles tapped her hand playfully with a paw and with a start she came back to the present. A tear traced down her cheek and she brushed it away impatiently, wishing it was as easy to erase the painful ache under her ribs. Her eyes went to the clock, and with a gasp of dismay she realised how long she had been wandering along the byways of the past.

She tipped the cat off her lap and raced upstairs. In less than half an hour Roxby would be here. She snatched up the outfit she planned to wear, her thoughts still with Jim and the way he had betrayed her with his secretary.

She paused, a hairpin in her hand, her reflection in the mirror showing blue eyes bright with outrage. Pushing the pin firmly in place, she exclaimed with muted fury, 'The arrogant, immoral bastard! Trying to seduce me, when he's engaged to that hussy Juliette.'

She had time to think of all the cold, contemptuous things she wished she'd said instead of giving in to him, and then Roxby rang the bell.

CHAPTER SIX

ALEXANDRA was adamant that when she next ran into Jim she would freeze him with chilly hauteur. Yet all the same she was relieved that in the days which followed no white BMW appeared outside her house, and she was grateful that Ellen mentioned when she was likely to encounter him again.

Her grandmother was flying out from Heathrow in ten days' time for a fortnight's holiday in Jersey, staying with friends. Jim had offered to drive her to the airport to catch the evening flight. Forewarned, Alexandra thought, was forearmed.

Her confidence might have been borne out if she hadn't met him again sooner than she had expected, and furthermore, in the company of Juliette. A difficult case she'd been working on had been won in court on a point of law which she had been astute enough to seize on. Roxby had been rather dampening in his congratulations, and she decided, as he had a Round Table meeting that evening, that she would celebrate her success with Ellen by having dinner at one of the best London hotels.

They chose a table for two in a corner of the elegant fourth-floor dining-room, as Ellen always liked to have a commanding position in any restaurant.

'What a treat this is,' Ellen smiled as she looked out at the vista of lights that showed beyond the panoramic windows. 'I sometimes forget when I'm cosily at home in the evening what a hub of activity London is at night.'

Below, the traffic streamed past incessantly, but inside there was no sound of it. The babel of conversation and the tinkle of crockery were muted by the expanse of thick carpeting. A selection of gently romantic music provided by the pianist at the grand piano added charm to the opulent setting. The panelled walls rose to a ceiling hung with chandeliers, and on a table in the centre of the dining-room was an enormous bowl massed with peonies, irises, roses and carnations.

'They've just got a new chef,' Alexandra remarked as they studied the menu, 'and the fish is marvellous.'

'In which case,' Ellen said, 'I'll have the Dover sole.'

'And what do you say to a bottle of champagne?' Alexandra asked.

Her grandmother's obvious pleasure was adding to her own enjoyment of the evening, which simply flew. They were lingering over coffee and eating mint chocolates when she looked up to see Jim walk into the dining-room.

'I don't believe it,' she muttered in a fierce undertone.

Puzzled, Ellen turned her head to follow Alexandra's gaze.

'Why, there's Jim,' she announced, pleased, before asking, 'Who's the pretty brunette with him?'

'Juliette Stanton,' Alexandra said between clenched teeth. 'Oh hell, they've seen us! Of all the most miserable luck . . .'

'Alexandra dear, I do think you're over-reacting a little,' Ellen chided gently as Jim, his hand at Juliette's elbow came over to their table.

Three years had only enhanced Juliette's slim, subtle beauty. She was wearing a silk blouse under a scarlet bolero-style jacket with a matching knee-length skirt that drew attention to her chorus-line legs. Her lustrous dark brown hair fell softly around her shoulders, emphasising her classical features. As always, her make-up was perfect, a hint of bronze colouring her high cheekbones, her Mona Lisa type smile made more seductive by a scarlet lipstick.

Carefully Alexandra moved her wineglass aside before the temptation to dash the contents in Jim's face became an uncontrollable impulse. Immaculately dressed, he had all the magnetic confidence and charm a background of wealth and success gave a man, and her fury at his total lack of moral principles was heightened by her awareness of his attractiveness.

'Jim, what a surprise!' Ellen smiled.

'Isn't it?' Alexandra agreed crisply. 'And quite enough to make me wish we'd gone elsewhere.'

Her sharp tongue earned her a stern look from her grandmother.

'And there was I about to suggest we make a foursome,' Jim mocked urbanely before introducing Juliette to Ellen.

'Well, unfortunately you're a little late with your suggestion,' said Alexandra with tart sarcasm as she put her napkin on the table. 'We're just leaving.'

'We've been celebrating one of Alexandra's successes at work,' Ellen explained with a touch of pride.

'How nice,' Juliette commented, giving Alexandra a smile that held a stinging depth of cold contempt.

Stung by it, Alexandra wondered for how many more seconds her restraint would stand up to this degree of provocation.

'Well, I'll see you some other time,' Jim remarked easily.

'Not if I see you first.'

It was a petty remark, but pride called for her to have the last word. Instead, she was cheated even of that. Cuttingly Jim said, 'Don't jump to conclusions, Alex. I was speaking to Ellen.'

He and Juliette moved away, and the moment they were out of earshot Ellen said sharply, 'Really, Alexandra, what has got into you? I've never heard you be so appallingly rude!'

'You can count yourself lucky you didn't witness murder,' she said in a dark undertone that concealed how unsteady her voice was.

'I thought all passion was over between you and Jim when you divorced.'

'It was . . . and . . . and I don't want to talk about this.'

'Alexandra dear!' Ellen exclaimed in concern as she reached out to take her hand. 'You're close to tears.'

'No, I'm not,' she denied fiercely. 'It's . . . it's that cigar smoke from the next table. I . . . I'd better go and fix my mascara.'

Keeping her shoulders squared, she made her way briskly across the dining-room, fighting the strangling tightness in her throat. What was wrong with her that she was allowing Jim to devastate her like this? Not even the shock of encountering him with his mistress was enough to explain her riotous anger.

Inside the ladies' room, she sank down on one of the couches. It took several minutes before she could quieten the tumult of her thoughts. Rebuking herself for her behaviour helped her to master the weakness of tears. She smoothed a wisp of hair into her chignon in front of the mirror, and with her poise at least outwardly restored decided she was up to returning to the dining-room.

At that moment Juliette came in. Alexandra stiffened, and then with aloof dignity made to walk past her. Her eyes were hard and her mouth set with the effort of controlling her emotions. Juliette stepped in front of her, barring her way.

'You really are something, aren't you?' she spat.

Alexandra froze to the spot.

'I don't have anything to say to you, Juliette,' she answered icily.

'I'm surprised,' Juliette jeered. 'When we stopped at your table, you were doing so well with the caustic comments. I thought perhaps it was a talent you'd perfected at law school.'

Alexandra ignored the cheap remark, but Juliette, refusing to allow her to leave, grabbed hold of her wrist as she swept on, 'I used to have some respect for you. Now I see you're just a workaholic iceberg who couldn't even keep her husband happy!'

So even in bed she'd failed to please Jim. She felt so groggy with pain, her pride so wounded, that in her desperate unhappiness she said with terse bitterness, 'You've had your victory coming here tonight with Jim. Let that satisfy you without further insulting me.'

'Insulting you? I haven't started yet.'

'Take your hands off me,' Alexandra demanded, erupting in a sudden explosion of wrath. 'I said take your hands *off* me, unless you want to be in court for assault!'

Juliette, jolted at being suddenly confronted by such an outraged fury, promptly did as she was told. Her eyes as dark as sapphires, Alexandra swept past her, returning to the dining-room, where she paced immediately over to Jim's table.

'You tell that hussy you're engaged to she'd better not *ever* speak to me like that again,' she began in a voice that shook with suppressed passion.

Jim's eyes narrowed. She should have had the advantage over him as she was the one who was standing, but with Jim those sort of rules never seemed to hold.

'Well, you surprise me,' he said sarcastically. 'Powder-room chat. Whoever would have thought Juliette could make you lose your cool? You'd better tell me exactly what was said.'

'I suggest you ask your fiancée. Doubtless she'll enjoy recounting it, since the two of you seem to discuss everything, including the fact that you found me an iceberg in bed!'

'No,' he said, a ferocity equal to hers in his voice. 'There Juliette's got it wrong. You were so hot in bed, it makes me wonder how that tame solicitor you're engaged to keeps you satisfied.'

'You just leave Roxby out of it!'

'If you ask me,' he said, getting to his feet, 'that's what you should do.'

'When I need your advice I'll ask for it!' snapped Alexandra. 'In fact, the more I see of you, the more staggered I am that our marriage lasted even two years!'

She turned abruptly and walked away, feeling his rapier-keen gaze between her shoulder-blades, and surprised at how much the short, blazing exchange had helped ease the rage inside her.

Immersing herself in her work the next day also helped her to recover from her brush with Juliette. Alexandra's office was on the fourth floor of a sedate Portland stone building that fronted on to the busy main road. Not far from the Strand, the suite of offices fitted perfectly with the law firm's venerable image.

She had spent most of the morning researching into previous rulings which would act as precedents for a case Roxby was handling. He had asked her for her summary by the end of the afternoon, but as she had finished it she thought she might as well hand it to his secretary in his outer office.

Collecting up her papers, she went out into the corridor and crossed the broad reception area with its pictures of the Inns of Court. Roxby's secretary was not at her desk when Alexandra went in, but seated on the leather sofa, idly leafing through one of the magazines provided, was the last person she could have expected to see—Jim.

He glanced up as she entered, but her surprise was so great that she didn't register that he was as unprepared for the encounter as she. He was wearing a charcoal suit,

dazzling white shirt, and a silk tie that showed both taste
and individuality, making Alexandra even more conscious
of his masculine charisma.

He immediately got to his feet on seeing her. His
advantage over her in height seemed to be yet another way
in which he threatened her. She glanced back through the
open doors to the empty reception area. Then, clutching
her papers to her blouse as if they were a defensive shield,
she began in a hissing whisper, 'This really is too much!
First last night, and now this. How dare you track me
down at work? I simply will not be hounded by you in this
way!'

'Track you down?' repeated Jim with a mixture of
incredulity and impatience. 'I had no idea you worked
here.'

'Oh, really?' she replied with chilly disbelief.

He looked down at her, his brows coming together as he
said,

'Good lord, woman, do you honestly imagine I'm
following you?' Maddening mockery came into his voice
as he went on, 'Admittedly, you were very tempting in that
pink robe the other day at your house, and I was a shade
overcome, but not so much so that I'm starting to tail you
to work.'

'I don't know how you've got the gall to refer to that
day, considering what an absolute cad you were!'

'What a very quaint vocabulary you're developing,' Jim
taunted. 'It must be Roxby's influence. I don't believe I've
ever been called a cad before.'

'That amazes me, because it sums you up perfectly! But
then I suppose you'd class the word fidelity as similarly
archaic.'

His eyes hardened as he said, 'Might I point out that
fidelity to Roxby was your problem on that particular
occasion?'

Alexandra felt herself colour hotly at his reminder of her shameful conduct, and with a renewed surge of anger she snapped, 'I'm talking about fidelity to Juliette—your fiancée!'

There was real venom in her voice and, watching her closely, Jim taunted lazily, 'I'd no idea you disliked Juliette so much. Or is it the idea of her taking your place that makes you so angry?'

'It's your despicable behaviour that makes me angry!' she snapped, her voice rising. She was finding that her ability to crush him was impeded by the fact that she had to look up at him so much. 'But there's one thing that I mean to get straight. In so far as you're engaged to Juliette, just what the hell are you doing here?'

'Then let me set your vain little mind at rest,' he replied sarcastically, his eyes mocking her. 'I'm not here to make a pass at you. Not that you don't look very enticing in that classy grey business suit, but right now I'm concerned with a legal problem that's cropped up between Global Freightways and another company. I have an appointment with a Mr W Robson, and as soon as that's over I'll be leaving.'

'Who . . . who did you say your appointment was with?' she asked, jolted out of her anger.

'A Mr W Robson. I'm waiting to see him now.'

'But . . . but that's Roxby,' Alexandra said in despair.

'*Roxby*?' he repeated disbelievingly.

'William's his first name, but he doesn't use it. He's called Roxby so he doesn't get confused with his father,' she began, before erupting, 'I don't know why I'm telling you all this! I don't believe a word of what you've just said. You're doing this deliberately, aren't you? With your macho pride, you just can't bear to see me happy with another man. It's fine for you to go off with someone else, but the same standards don't apply to me. I'm right, aren't

I? You're out to break up my engagement.'

'Stop being so neurotic,' ordered Jim. 'If I'd been as possessive as you're making out, you wouldn't have got your divorce in the first place.'

'Then if you're not trying to break up my engagement, why is it that lately I can't seem to move without falling over you?'

'Would you like me to have a word with Roxby and tell him I have no wicked designs on you, that even after our night together on Capri your virtue is still intact?' he mocked.

'Don't you *dare* mention Capri to him,' she breathed, glaring at him.

Jim's eyes narrowed. In the instant's silence Alexandra felt him studying her like a psychiatrist, probing and pondering.

'You mean you didn't tell him?' he taunted softly. 'What happened to your wonderfully honest relationship?'

'Oh, go to hell!' she snapped.

Jim caught hold of her arm and she started as though the live warmth of his touch scorched her even through her blouse. Immediately she dropped the sheaf of papers she was holding.

'Now look what you've done!' she exclaimed in annoyance as she bent to retrieve the scattered sheets.

'It's scarcely my fault if you jump six feet every time I so much as touch you,' Jim said caustically as he stooped to help her.

As he handed her a couple of sheets, she replied fiercely, 'Well, maybe I wouldn't if it wasn't for the fact that the moment you come near me, my life turns into one round of minor calamities!'

Whatever Jim had been about to say in answer to that was lost, for at that moment Roxby opened the door from his office. About to welcome Jim inside, he checked his greeting. Not the least bit discomfited, Jim straightened up leisurely, his hand at Alexandra's elbow as he helped her to her feet.

'Mr Logan?' Roxby began in his professionally pleasant manner. 'How do you do? I see you've . . . er . . . met my assistant, Ms Challoner.'

'Indeed I have,' said Jim, a hint of a smile tugging at his mouth that made Alexandra itch to slap him.

This was awkward enough, without Jim suddenly turning the situation into a joke. Touching her chignon lightly with her hand, she said, 'I . . . I dropped my papers.' She paused, and added with a little embarrassed laugh, 'By an amazing coincidence, Jim happens to be my ex-husband. Jim, I'd like you to meet my fiancé, Roxby Robson.'

She was conscious of a faint touch of pride at having so quickly recovered a semblance of poise. Roxby gave Jim an obviously appraising glance, and then offered his hand with an excess of amiability.

'As you say, darling, what a coincidence,' he said.

'Yes, small world,' Jim agreed in a straight-faced parody of Roxby's trite remark as he returned the robust handshake.

With an effort, Alexandra pretended to have missed the subtle gibe. She said, 'I've got an appointment with a client, so I'll leave the two of you to get down to business.'

'Nice to bump into you again, Alex,' Jim mocked gently. 'See you anon, I expect.'

This time she glowered at him. Damn him for ridiculing Roxby's manner of speaking *and* deliberately reminding her of the evening when she had kissed him so passionately!

She marched back into her office, threw her papers on to her desk and went over to the window. Folding her arms, she stared out, seeing the vivid green of the lime trees and the red tops of the buses as they went by. Still smarting at Jim's sarcastic mockery, she was glad she had a few minutes' grace till her client arrived. At the moment she felt too angry and harassed to resume the tasks of the afternoon. All she could think of was that Jim was now with Roxby.

She knew they wouldn't discuss her, yet just the same there was bound to be a bit of tentative preamble involving her before they began to talk business. It didn't improve her temper to realise that if she hadn't behaved so recklessly with Jim the other day at her house she wouldn't be feeling so fiery and ill at ease now.

She sat down at her desk and tapped a pencil against the blotter. For a few moments she wished she was both unattached and anywhere but in London. Then she wouldn't be in this impossible emotional tangle.

Abruptly she cut the thought short. There *was* no emotional tangle, she told herself firmly. She wanted her future linked with Roxby's and Jim out of her life, which he would be once he married Juliette. The prospect should have pleased her. Instead, when her secretary announced that her client had arrived, she was feeling unmistakably depressed.

Work made a welcome diversion. When her phone rang as she was showing her client out, she had temporarily forgotten Jim. She picked up the receiver to hear Roxby say, 'Alexandra, if you're free, I wonder if you could come along to my office for a minute.'

'Of course,' she answered with a smile.

Some day, when the two of them were married, she was going to look back and be faintly amused with herself for allowing Jim to make her so irritable and for ever having the vague premonition that something was going to go wrong between her and Roxby. She must get rid of this lurking fear that she couldn't make a happy, lasting relationship.

Certain that by now Jim would have left the building, she went into Roxby's office—only to be disappointed. He was still there, seated across the desk from her fiancé. He looked totally relaxed, but as always there was that latent quality about him that gave rise to the feeling that whatever aces were in the pack, he held them. She was conscious of his swarthy attractiveness. She was equally conscious, and tried not to be, of his masculine gaze on her slim legs, black stockings and demure court shoes.

'Ah, here you are,' Roxby announced.

Alexandra sat down beside his desk and crossed her legs. Refusing to allow Jim to unsettle her, she gave him a cool glance of uninterest. A curious tension flared for an instant as their eyes met, and then faded.

'Let me put you in the picture with regard to the case,' Roxby continued. 'It transpires that a company also in the export packing field has set up using Global Freightways' logo, with the consequent effect on loss of orders and company image and so on. I've been telling Mr Logan that you're very familiar with handling this sort of work.'

She murmured her agreement, bracing herself as she suddenly anticipated why Roxby had asked her to join them.

'I take it you've no objection to Alexandra handling the case?' asked Roxby.

Jim lifted a casual hand from the arm of his chair.

'No, none,' he said, his gaze meeting hers with the merest trace of a challenge.

Alexandra returned it coldly. She wouldn't have chosen a case that would bring her into contact with him, but their former connection was certainly no reason for her to turn it down. He clearly couldn't press any attentions on her in her office, and, even if he could, she was more than ready for him now. Proving that to both of them might even be salutary.

'Splendid,' said Roxby. 'Well then, Mr Logan, I'll leave you in Alexandra's very capable hands.'

An amused gleam came into Jim's hard brown eyes at her fiancé's turn of phrase. Determined that he was not going to view her as a potential source of entertainment, she said with telling briskness, 'I'll contact you in a few days' time, after I've written to the other side. I'm sure we'll have the matter resolved quite quickly.'

Catching her meaning, Jim smiled at her, an annoying smile, as though Roxby wasn't there. Hurriedly she dropped her gaze. Whatever her intention had been, communicating without words wasn't the most sensible of games to be indulging in when she was trying her hardest to forget the rapport the two of them had once shared.

Jim stood up, and with great affability Roxby shook his hand again. Alexandra also got to her feet, her manner still quite placid, even if her eyes were not. Roxby's attitude of broad-minded geniality towards her ex-husband was beginning to get on her nerves.

'By the way,' said Jim, seemingly as an afterthought, 'I've just bought a house in Rickmansworth. I'm giving a housewarming party on Saturday. I don't know if you and Alexandra would like to look in some time during the evening? If so . . . Juliette and I would be very pleased to see you.'

'Most kind of you,' Roxby murmured. 'We'd be delighted.'

'Fine,' said Jim, adding to Alexandra, 'Ellen will give you the address.'

While Roxby escorted him to the door, she perched on the edge of the desk with a sense of utter disbelief. The very last thing she wanted was to be entertained by her ex-husband and the woman who had broken up her marriage. The moment Jim had gone she began, 'Why on *earth* did you say we'd go to Jim's housewarming?'

'You have to admit it did put me in rather a difficult position.'

'Difficult, how? Surely you could have said we had other plans?'

'And I would have done, but I thought you might want me to accept.'

'*Accept*?' she repeated incredulously.

'Yes,' Roxby defended himself. 'From what you've always said, you and your husband have stayed on friendly terms. I thought if I turned the invitation down it might have looked as if I was being rather petty and jealous.' He paused, and then added rather as if was clarifying a point with the counsel for the prosecution, 'I assume I have no reason to be jealous.'

'Of course you don't,' Alexandra denied quickly. 'That's the most ridiculous thing to say!'

This was the closest she and Roxby had ever come to having an argument, and the irony of it was that it was over her ex-husband, who could go to the devil for all she cared. She went on, 'I wouldn't be marrying you if I had any feelings left for Jim.'

'That's what I thought,' said Roxby, patting her hand. 'And after all, we don't have to stay long at the party if it isn't our scene. I take it Juliette's his wife?'

'No, she's his fiancée,' Alexandra answered a shade shortly.

'I see,' Roxby commented, adding, 'Actually, you know, I could tell Jim's not your type. The two of you couldn't have been well-matched at all. I suppose it was a case of opposites attracting.'

'Yes,' she agreed wryly, 'I suppose it was.'

CHAPTER SEVEN

As SHE dressed for the party on Saturday, Alexandra found herself dwelling on her first marriage. Of all the emotions Jim's infidelity had aroused, the loss of trust and the destruction of self-esteem had been the most permanent. However much she tried to hate him for his betrayal, always underneath was the sense of self-doubt. How had she failed him that he'd preferred Juliette to her?

She glanced at herself critically in the full-length mirror. The slinky silk jersey dress she had chosen made her look slim and sophisticated. It was sleeveless and showed off her warm tan, while the turquoise print brought out the blueness of her eyes. Already she felt more in a fighting spirit. Despite the power of seduction Juliette had, Jim was going to see what he had given up. And, furthermore, that hussy he intended marrying might as well sense that she'd better not come out with any more malicious remarks!

It was a beautiful evening. The dusk was just coming on and the sky was flushed on the horizon with the glow of sunset. The view as Roxby drove down the steep Rickmansworth hill showed a sweeping vista of green fields and merged into uncertain blues on the horizon. The restful scenery made it easier for Alexandra to pretend she was equal to the evening that lay ahead.

They found the tree-lined avenue where Jim now lived without difficulty, and parked a short distance from his partly timbered house that was built with strong, clean lines. From the number of cars parked along the kerb, the party was a big one and already she could hear the throb of music.

Jim showed them into the large split-level lounge. With patio doors open on to the garden, it was full of talk and laughter. Although it was still early in the evening, already the party had a relaxed mood, and on the patio several couples were dancing to a strong disco beat.

'What will you have to drink?' asked Jim, raising his voice slightly above the babel of conversation. 'Your usual, Alex? And how about you, Roxby?'

She tried not to feel annoyed by Jim's easy familiarity with her. She was trying equally hard not to be too obvious in her glance round the crowded lounge in her attempt to locate Juliette. But it was clear from Jim's next remark that he'd guessed her thoughts. His dark eyes mocking her, he said, 'Unfortunately Juliette's been delayed. She won't be here till quite a bit later.'

'What a pity,' she answered, giving him a distant little smile.

He needn't think he was going to get a rise out of her this evening. Her emotions were far too securely battened down. What was more, with no Juliette to divert her attention, this was a first-class opportunity to show Jim just how good her relationship with her fiancé was. If anyone was to be stung by jealousy tonight, she meant it to be her ex-husband.

Tugging Roxby gently by the arm, she said with a radiant smile, 'Darling, I can't stand still to this kind of music. Why don't we dance?'

They went outside to Jagger and Bowie's 'Dancing in the Street'. Disco dancing wasn't really Roxby's scene. Somehow it didn't match up with his personality and smart suit, and she knew he would rather have waited until later when the music was gentler and more nostalgic.

Catching hold of her hand, he twirled her towards him as Jim and a slim blonde came out to dance on the patio.

Seeing him, Alexandra stiffened, and Roxby, who had intended twisting her round under his arm, merely succeeded in tying her up in a cramped little knot close to his chest. She let go of his hand quickly, hoping Jim hadn't caught sight of her comic performance. The glance he gave her told her he had missed nothing and, to reinforce it, he even gave her a slight wink. She gave him a hard, unappreciative look. She was getting a little tired of his subtle mockery.

'We'll have to practise some more if we're going to get the hang of this,' Roxby commented with a laugh.

'Actually I'm getting out of breath,' she lied. 'Shall we go back inside?'

All week she had fretted over this party, wishing there was some way she could get out of it. Now, having discovered that it would give her immense satisfaction to needle Jim, she was strengthened by defiance. She was quite glad, in fact, that Roxby hadn't turned down the invitation. Jim might as well see the evidence of how lucky she counted herself to have found such a loyal, monogamous man.

Some of the couples at the party she knew from the time she'd been married. She had to admire Roxby for the imperturbable way he immediately made conversation with them. Not only was he urbane, but he was as solid as a rock.

It was dark outside by now, and the long garden was softly illuminated with coloured floodlights. Someone evidently decided it was time to shift the mood by putting a slower record on the stereo. Her fiancé suggested that they dance to it.

The patio was full of romantic shadows. Roxby held her firmly as he moved with her in a waltz. There was, she told herself, something very reassuring about being in his arms. But the contentment didn't last long. She was startled by

Jim, who put a hand on Roxby's shoulder.

'Tina's one of our trainees,' he said as he introduced the teenager to them. 'She's too shy to admit it, Roxby, but she's longing to dance with you. You see, she can't waltz and she's convinced you could teach her.'

'I just love these old-fashioned dances,' Tina put in with a giggle. 'They look so sort of elegant.'

As though the matter was settled, with one hand Jim guided Tina deftly towards Roxby while he slipped an arm round Alexandra's waist.

'I can't think when we last danced together,' he remarked blandly as he drew her into his arms.

'*Jim*,' she said warningly, mistakenly taking the shiver that went through her for apprehension that he was going to mention Capri.

'You don't really think I'd give you away, do you?' he taunted, before commenting, 'Roxby seems to be having a good time.'

She turned her head to see the cause of his dry amusement. Her fiancé was counting the three beats, looking mildly irritated, while Tina was in gales of laughter and treading on his feet. Determined Jim would not get her on the defensive, she said, 'I think he's quite enjoyed meeting some of our old friends. In fact, I very much admire him for the way he's handled this evening.'

Something flickered in Jim's dark eyes. She despised herself for hoping it was jealousy, as his easy-going enquiry proved her wrong.

'And how are you enjoying yourself?'

The music seemed to be drugging her. She had always liked the sweet sadness of the hit 'Solitaire'. Pulling herself together, she said stoically, 'I'm having a lovely evening, but then, you always knew how to throw a party.'

She'd been glad of their conversation to weaken the silken thread of the music that was wrapping them together. The problem was that the spell was too strong, demanding a communication deeper than words. Without her realising it, a poignant sentimentality was stealing over her.

Jim enfolded her more closely, bringing her body into an intimate fit against his. Her movements were guided so perfectly by his that it seemed only natural to move her hands from his shoulders to link them behind his neck. After all, could there really be any harm just this once in letting him mould her to him, in allowing herself to feel close to him again?

When the evocative music finally faded, for an instant it was like coming back from a dream. Jim released her, taking her hand in his before she could shake off her nostalgic mood.

'While we've got a few minutes together, let me show you over the rest of the house.'

He had led her through the patio doors before she remembered the gulf that now separated them.

'I've no particular inclination to look over your love-nest, thank you,' she told him with cool hostility.

'Or is it that you're afraid to be alone with me?' he asked.

Conscious of the warmth of his hand against her back, she answered, her voice scathing because deep down she knew there was a certain degree of truth in what he'd said, 'That line's as old as the hills.'

'Old, but to the point,' he replied as he guided her firmly across the lounge, 'considering what happened the last time we were alone together.'

Alexandra halted, facing him with antagonism.

'I made a mistake that evening at my house! Instead of letting Roxby leave when he called, I should have told him my ex-husband was molesting me and he'd have pulverised you!'

Jim burst into laughter, making her eyes blaze. He caught hold of her wrist as she was about to sweep away from him in fury.

'Don't be difficult, Alex,' he said, mirth still in his voice. 'I'm trying to say I'm sorry.'

'Then you're trying in a very funny way!'

But just the same, surprised by his remark, she let him lead her into the hall without resistance. Free from the constraint of other people, he released her and went on, 'Listen, you looked very enticing that day at your place and events got out of hand. I know what you think, but I'm not out to wreck things for you.'

'Well, that's very noble of you,' she said tartly. 'Of course, I suppose you have no doubts that if it weren't for your sense of male camaraderie with Roxby, you could succeed in seducing me?'

She caught the glimmer of amusement in his eyes and felt she would choke on it. But the next instant he was perfectly serious as he told her, 'Truly, Alex, when I said I hoped you'd be happy, I meant it.'

She looked back at him, her gaze becoming less turbulent. Then, prepared to call a temporary cease-fire if he was, she said with a smile, 'In which case, I would be interested in a tour of the house.'

'OK, let's start with the upstairs.'

She followed him up the luxuriously carpeted staircase to the galleried landing. Tactfully he did not show her the master bedroom, and she was glad. To have seen Juliette's toiletries and lingerie among his things would have pushed her restraint too far.

They went back downstairs and into the kitchen. Streamlined with blue and white fitted units, it looked out over the road. Alexandra glanced round and said, 'I'm running a little short of adjectives after seeing the upstairs, but the kitchen's a dream.'

Jim smiled at her approval. It deepened the attractive lines of his face. His white shirt was open at the neck. She could see the strong, tanned column of his throat and the faint shading of hair that she knew grew in a dark V down his chest. She felt a stir of sexual awareness and hurriedly averted her gaze from his.

There was an open letter on the worktop beside her. From it had spilled out some photos of a baby who was gurgling happily at the camera. Conscious of a need for a diversion, she picked them up.

'That's my little nephew,' Jim remarked, coming to stand beside her so they could look at the photos together. 'I'm glad that Tricia's settled down so happily now.'

His sister was almost ten years younger than he was. Married to a diplomat, she was currently living with her husband in Geneva.

'Ellen told me she'd had a little boy,' Alexandra smiled, her momentary weakness of a minute ago forgotten. 'He's absolutely gorgeous. He's called Jim too, isn't he?'

Jim laughed and said, 'Yes, I was rather touched by that.'

'She was lucky to be able to live with you when she was going through that bumpy patch,' Alexandra commented.

She knew that Tricia had been only seventeen when her mother had died. Their father had married again very quickly and, finding a stepmother hard to accept, Tricia had gone through a very wild stage when drink and even drugs had been a problem. That had all been before Alexandra had known Jim. When she had met his sister, Tricia had just finished a course in modern languages and was on the point of getting engaged. With a less caring and protective older brother, Alexandra very much doubted that things would have worked out so well for her. Jim was just the sort of man for a crisis, his easy style masking an undertone of strength and firmness.

He was ideal brother material. Some day, she was certain, he would make the most wonderful father. Her heart contracted with a pang that was almost pain.

'I suppose you and Roxby are planning on having a family?' asked Jim.

'No, we're not, as it happens,' she said, her voice marked with a light unconcern that didn't match her mood. Looking at the photos of the adorably chubby baby with Jim seemed to be awakening in her regrets she thought she'd long since abandoned.

'That seems a shame,' Jim commented. 'You'd be good with kids. In fact, I thought you and I would have some of our own.'

Alexandra had too, when she had married him. And if Jim had stayed faithful to her there would have been nothing that would have brought her greater happiness than to have given him a child.

'Well, fate decreed otherwise,' she said as she handed him back the photos.

At that moment Juliette came into the kitchen. She was wearing a short, flamboyant dress, cut to show off her shapely legs, and her dark hair was a mass of tousled curls. When Alexandra had dressed aiming to eclipse her, she hadn't reckoned that Juliette would look quite so Carmen-like. She felt a riot of emotions, all of them turbulent, and struggled to suppress them.

'I'm sorry I'm later than I said,' Juliette began.

'Any later and I'd have organised a search party,' smiled Jim, putting an arm round her waist.

This further provocation, when Alexandra was already fighting to overcome an acute sense of being completely outclassed by Juliette's sultry beauty, was almost too much. Before her poise splintered, she said a shade coolly, 'Well, I think it's time Roxby and I were leaving. Thanks, Jim, for a pleasant evening.'

'I'm glad you could come,' he answered.

To her immense surprise he kissed her twice on the cheek, continental fashion. Juliette seemed to think nothing of it, and Alexandra felt a surge of anger that all it took was a casual goodbye from him to set her heart thudding.

She was thoughtful as she and Roxby strolled back to his car. The dark sky was lofty and cloudless, showing a brilliant moon, while the night was filled with the sultry fragrance of pollen. She refused to allow Jim to upset her, or to allow a faint restlessness to surface. And she certainly wasn't going to start playing with the idea of what a baby would mean to her. Roxby wasn't going to change his mind about not wanting a family. She reminded herself that she liked her job and was happy with her fiancé. To want anything more was to be a child crying for the moon.

CHAPTER EIGHT

A WEEK later the solicitors working for the other side contacted her with proposals which would be acceptable to their clients if Global Freightways would agree. She doubted that Jim would accept them, but she phoned him anyway.

'Hi, Alex,' he began crisply. 'I'm afraid you've caught me at a busy time. I'm just leaving for Luton to sort out a problem with a freight consignment at the airport. Is it urgent?'

'Not especially. I've got some proposals for you to look over.'

'Good,' he commented. 'We're making some headway, then.'

'Not as much as I'd like. I really need to see you to discuss them with you. Could you come into the office some time this week?'

'No, this week's out, I'm afraid,' he said. He paused and then asked, 'You couldn't drop them round at my place this evening, could you? I'll be home by about eight. If not, it's going to have to wait until next week.'

She hesitated and he added mockingly, 'Juliette's in Hull at the moment. Knowing your dislike of her, perhaps that makes a difference. You needn't worry that you're going to run into her.'

'Juliette has got nothing to do with it,' she lied coldly. 'I was merely trying to think what I've got planned for this evening.'

In fact, she'd got nothing planned. Roxby was away in Birmingham covering for a colleague who had been taken ill in the middle of a case. Jim's request was perfectly reasonable. Quite proud that she could treat him at last in a cool, professional way, she said, 'Yes, all right. I'll see you at eight.'

He must have got back from Luton later than he'd expected, because he answered the door to her with his hair still wet from the shower and with his shirt undone. She found she was staring at his powerfully muscled chest, caught herself quickly, and began in a rush, 'I've brought the papers I mentioned. I'm sorry if I'm early. I——'

'Fine,' he interrupted, as though her nervous chatter amused him. 'Come on in.'

He stood back to allow her inside and started to button his shirt. Alexandra was glad now she hadn't changed out of her smart linen suit. She had thought of it, but then had decided that as this was a business meeting it was safer to look the part. Seeing him half naked and in jeans had made her realise it was a wise decision.

She sat down on the sofa and handed him the proposals. Jim paced with them towards the window. His hair was darkened with water and as always, there was something pagan and pantherish about his stride.

'No, I'm not accepting this,' he said as he turned back to her. 'Altering the spelling of the company name simply isn't far-reaching enough. You can tell them it's no deal, Alex.'

'If I can get them to agree to arbitration, would you be happy with that? It would keep costs down.'

'Yes, try it,' he agreed. 'But make it clear that if they want a court case they can have it.'

She discussed some of the finer points of the case with him, and then stood up to leave.

'Stay and have coffee while you're here,' Jim suggested.

She hadn't intended to, but talking over the case with him had made the atmosphere between them seem almost harmless.

'Just a quick cup,' she agreed.

'I take it you've eaten?'

'No, I'll cook something when I get home.'

'Have dinner here. I've got steak in the fridge.'

'I'm not that hungry,' she replied pointedly.

'Still worried I have designs on your virtue?' he mocked.

He reached out casually and caught hold of her by the arm. She started at his touch, struggling as he drew her level with his chest.

'When are you going to stop being so jumpy with me?' he asked with lazy amusement.

'When you learn to keep your hands off me,' she said a shade breathlessly.

She pushed angrily against him. He freed her and she glared at him, annoyed that she had let him see how easily he could unsettle her. Why did she let him get her in a panic? Trying to recover her poise, she said defiantly, 'The only reason I'm a little jumpy with you is that I don't feel all that comfortable about being here.'

Jim's dark eyes searched hers. No eyes had ever searched hers the way his did. They were quizzical, interested and formidably shrewd.

'What's wrong with your being here?' he asked. 'You had a perfectly legitimate reason to call.'

'I know I did,' she said. 'But it still feels wrong.'

She realised suddenly she didn't want to explain further because she wasn't quite sure what she might end up saying. Annoyed that she had confessed so much, she went on crossly, 'What I mean is, I'm sure it's not usual for an ex-husband and wife to keep seeing each other the way we have lately.'

'Well, we weren't exactly a usual couple even when we were married,' Jim commented. 'The irony is that then we scarcely had any time together.'

'Oh, so it's *my* fault we split up!' she flared, before realising she had no intention of starting a post-mortem on their marriage.

'My, fiery this evening, aren't we?'

Alexandra swept him an angry look and, snapping her briefcase shut, was about to head for the door when he caught hold of her again.

'Alex, calm down,' he ordered. 'I'm not trying to provoke you.'

'Really? I think you do nothing but deliberately provoke me.'

'No, I don't, but it might be an idea for you to think about why you're afraid to stay and have dinner with me.'

She stared at him, her eyes very blue. Very distinctly she told him, 'I'm not afraid to stay. I don't know why you've got it into your head that I'm still attracted to you. Beyond a certain antipathy, Jim, there's nothing between us.' He didn't contradict her, but the way he looked at her made her feel the need to match her actions to her words. Rashly she added, 'So yes, I will stay and have dinner.'

For once she felt she'd got the upper hand with him. She knew far too much about him to be in any real danger by being alone with him and, furthermore, it wouldn't hurt his male ego to realise it.

She followed him into the kitchen, and while he started the meal she made the side salads and laid the table in the dining-room. She took the candles from the sideboard, and with a touch of bravado lit them and placed them on the table. Jim came in with the meal and poured the wine, a full-bodied claret.

'You used to like your steak medium rare. Have your tastes changed?'

'No, my tastes are just the same,' she said coolly.

'We'll drink to that,' he said, lifting his glass to her in a slight salute. 'To days gone by and shared tastes.'

Alexandra sipped the wine, its warmth relaxing her. Or perhaps it was Jim who was responsible for her lowering her guard. For once he seemed to have no desire to light the fuse to her temper, and with a slight pang she thought what good company he was.

Only once did they get on to a difficult topic. Jim had been talking about the trip he'd got lined up. He was flying out to Switzerland shortly for three weeks. It was a combination of both business and pleasure, and he was planning on visiting his sister in Geneva for a few days. Alexandra assumed that Juliette was going with him, but didn't ask.

Tricia had married a man several years older than she was, and speaking about him Jim said, 'It seems some women need a father figure in their lives. I suppose that's why you picked up with Roxby.'

'Father figure?' she echoed indignantly, all the more ready to flare up because she was thinking of Juliette. 'Roxby isn't a father figure. He's only five years older than you!'

'I didn't mean to put you on the defensive,' mocked Jim. 'Come on, let's take our coffee into the lounge.'

Jim poured her a Tia Maria. Twilight had invaded the large room. Outside the garden had faded, the colours darkening till the view in the distance was tinged with lavender.

Sitting chatting with him in the dusk reminded her of the early days of their marriage. She kicked her shoes off, enjoying the music that Jim had put on the stereo. It was Dvorak's *New World Symphony*, and the plaintive cadences seemed to complement her nostalgic mood. She leaned her head back against the sofa and closed her eyes, thinking of the many good times the two of them had shared.

When he took the coffee-cup from her, she started a

little.

'I think I woke you up.'

'I was miles away,' she admitted.

'Then let me pour you some more coffee to wake you up,' said Jim. 'I can't have you going to sleep on me.'

'I was only daydreaming,' she said, sitting up and slipping her shoes back on, 'but yes, I will have more coffee.'

'Do you remember that old chap who nodded off at that concert we went to?' Jim asked as he joined her on the sofa.

Her eyes kindled attractively.

'Oh, yes,' she said with a laugh, taking the cup he handed her.

They had been at a concert of chamber music. They had only been married a couple of months, and Olivia had given them the tickets as an unexpected present. She took a sip of coffee, set the cup down on the table beside her and added, 'I watched his head go down lower and lower, but I never expected him to wake up suddenly with that loud grunt.'

'Yes, it was quite effective,' Jim commented, amused, 'especially as it was in the quietest bit of the music. The string quartet nearly stopped in its tracks!'

Alexandra started to laugh at the memory. She remembered how she had begun to giggle, and the more she had tried to stop the more hopeless it had become, till she had shaken with suppressed merriment.

'You disgraced me,' said Jim with mock affront. 'I had to take you out.'

'I know,' she laughed. 'I just couldn't help it—it was so damn funny! But the concert wasn't quite right for us, anyway, was it? Mother always thinks I'm more highbrow than I am.'

'Really? I thought the tickets were aimed at me.'

'Oh, Jim, don't!' she laughed. 'Mother meant well.'

'And then,' he went on with a smile, 'there was that little Italian restaurant we went to afterwards.'

'Don't remind me,' she put in. 'It was where I nearly got the spaghetti down my dress.'

'I must admit I've never seen anyone tackle spaghetti with a spoon before!'

'That was the waiter's suggestion,' she said indignantly. 'Anyway, it was lucky we met him.'

'Because he taught you how to eat spaghetti?'

'No,' she laughed, 'because he started talking about his home in Stresa. It was because he made it sound so idyllic you booked up that fortnight for us on the Italian lakes. Have you forgotten?'

Jim smiled at her.

'No, I haven't forgotten,' he said quietly.

Her gaze went to his. Suddenly the air seemed dense with hidden static, and she couldn't break the spell. The lamplight emphasised the strong planes of Jim's face, making her more aware of its character. The moments dragged on before he said, 'We had a room overlooking the lake, and at night you could hear the water lapping the shore.'

It was a mistake to have started to wander down the paths of the past with him. Wistfulness clutched at her. That holiday in Italy had been one of the happiest of her life. She thought of the way the lights had shimmered on the blackness of the lake. The sultry breeze had come in through the open balcony doors, bringing with it the faint fragrance of the oleanders.

Suddenly she couldn't stop the memories coming back of the way he had made love to her. She smiled faintly, her heart tightening.

'We had our moments, didn't we?' she whispered.

'We did,' he murmured.

He put his arm round her, she thought intending only to draw her close, but at that moment she looked up at him. Their eyes locked, making her skin tingle and her heart race wildly in sudden anticipation at what she knew must inevitably happen.

'For old times' sake,' Jim breathed huskily as he bent his head.

Shakily Alexandra murmured his name as his lips found hers. His kiss was gentle, but the shock of excitement and pleasure that went through her made her wind her arms tightly about his neck. Nothing was real except the past. His kiss deepened and she returned it, unable to resist the deep sense of belonging to him. It was a golden moment and she wanted it to last forever.

When at last he raised his head, she felt almost dizzy. Her body ached with a sense of loneliness. Her eyes, lost and intense, met his, the silent message that flew between them filling her with a crazy recklessness. She had to feel his mouth, sweet and demanding, on hers again, had to feel his body tense and aroused against hers.

'Alex,' he muttered harshly.

He crushed her to him, his hand slipping fluently beneath her blouse as he arched her to him, kissing her with a fierce, passionate demand that made desire flame wildly inside her. She seemed to have waited an eternity to feel him mould her against his strong body again.

Her breasts were pressed against the hardness of his chest, the sensation shatteringly erotic. Excitement was pulsing through her as an elemental force, and she kissed him back with a feverishness as though she could never feel close enough to him.

She broke the kiss with a sudden gasp of pleasure as his hand cupped the softness of her breast. A rush of colour came into her face. Faintly her mind tried to recall her to sanity, and she closed her eyes and whispered with a husky moan, 'Jim . . . no . . .'

'Oh, you intoxicate me!' he breathed as he pressed passionate kisses down her throat.

He eased her blouse from her shoulders, and she shivered as he bent to kiss the swell of her breasts. Tears came to her closed eyes as the need to have him make love to her overpowered her. It was too late now to fight against the very virility she had warned herself against. Without meaning to, she slid her hands beneath his shirt, delighting in the iron feel of him and wanting no barrier between his skin and hers.

'You're beautiful,' he murmured as he found the clasp to her bra and freed her breasts.

His gaze held hers for an instant before he let it sweep over her, setting every nerve clamouring with excitement. With a low growl of desire he pressed his mouth to her skin, following the path his eyes had taken. His tongue circled her nipple and she cried out, tangling her fingers mindlessly in his crisp hair, while her heart thundered against his thirsty mouth.

She felt his hand stroke the smoothness of her thigh, but he had dismantled her defences too completely for her to even think of resisting him. When he swept her up into his arms and began to carry her upstairs into the bedroom she was already on fire for him.

His knowing hands had already obliterated the years she had spent without him. Reason didn't exist in this dizzy pleasure. She was his woman and she belonged to him.

He laid her on the bed, leaning over her to kiss her as though he was appeasing an eternity of hunger. The pins slipped from her hair. He slid his hands the whole length of her, travelling down her slim back and continuing over her hips, removing her panties as they went by. Trembling with desire, Alexandra pressed her lips feverishly to his shoulder before running her hands lovingly over his strong back.

Not even when he left her side to take off his jeans did an instant's sanity return. Instead she could only gaze at him, her breath catching in her throat at the beautiful power of his man's body. His shoulders were broad and she let her eyes travel from them down his chest to his long, muscular legs. She opened her arms as he lowered himself into her embrace.

'I want you,' she breathed raggedly.

'Say it again,' he demanded as he pressed kisses down the line of her throat to between her breasts.

But her heart was beating too wildly for her to say anything, except to gasp his name as his mouth captured her nipple.

Jim had always been an expert lover, kindling her desire with his sensitive hands until they were both lost in the conflagration of passion. She moaned deep in her throat as he made her aware of every inch of his strong, aroused body. His mouth girdled her waist with kisses before he kissed her lips again, his hands pushing back her wildly falling hair. Yearning ran like fire along her veins. Already her nipples were teased to peaks of taut, exquisite pleasure, and she turned her head on the pillow as Jim began to caress her with still greater intimacy.

His body seemed to be enveloping her, his deep, husky voice hypnotising her as he told her how she enchanted him. The sensations he was arousing in her were almost more than she could bear. She gave a gasping moan as his body covered hers, waves of wanting sweeping over her in a frantic crescendo.

She wasn't even aware that she cried out that she loved him in the instant before he entered her. A tide of sexual pleasure roared through her as she felt the thrust of his penetration. Moving with him in the ultimate embrace, she clung helplessly to his shuddering body. She gave a bewildered cry, stiffening suddenly. And then, as her body was showering her with delight, he too reached the summit. Tumbling with him through the waterfall of desire, she heard his deep groan of fulfilment.

Afterwards she lay completely spent, her eyes closed and her heart still pounding fiercely. She was filled with a rapture that made her almost want to cry. Jim had claimed her body and spirit and, still caught in the web of the past, reality didn't exist. She stirred and reached for his hand and, as she did so, he drew her into his arms. She rested her head against his chest, feeling his hands gentle on her slim back as he cherished her in love's afterglow. Her skin felt like silk from his touch, and she was half drugged with a sweet tiredness.

'I didn't think I could have forgotten how incredible you are,' he murmured.

She raised her head and smiled into his eyes before touching his lips caressingly with her finger.

'Nobody's ever made me feel the way you do,' she breathed with a contented sigh.

Jim smiled back and, enveloped by his protective tenderness, Alexandra laid her head against his chest again, feeling the steady beating of his heart. Curled close to his warm body, within moments she had drifted into a deep, fulfilled sleep.

It was half-light when she woke, and the room was dim with shadows. She stirred a little and then flickered her eyes open. Despite the sensuous languor that rippled through her, a faint expression of puzzlement crossed her face. The window was in the wrong place. Suddenly she realised this was not her bedroom, this was not her bed and, furthermore, she was not alone in it.

Jim's arm, heavy with slumber, was across her naked waist. She gave an involuntary gasp of dismay, twisted a

little and stared at him asleep beside her. His hair was dark
against the pillow and his face, even in sleep, had a
forcefulness of character.

The memories of the raging tide of their passionate
lovemaking came surging into her mind and she tensed,
horrorstruck. Jim sighed deeply, his breath fanning on to
her skin as he drew her closer. Colour flamed in her face as
she felt his naked body against hers. Trembling, she tried
to extricate herself from his embrace without waking him.

She eased her leg out from between his and then slid
gently towards her side of the bed. He stirred, and she
froze for an instant before slithering off the mattress.

Her heart was pounding and her mouth was dry.
Heavens, what had she done? In the dimness she groped
round the room for her clothes. She couldn't find her
blouse or her bra. She seemed to remember that she had
been divested of those even before Jim had carried her
upstairs.

Slipping her petticoat over her head, she cast another
look at where he lay asleep, her throat tightening. The
sheet had slipped down to show the broad expanse of his
back, the shadows heightening the powerful lines of his
relaxed body. Even in the morning the aura of his potent
masculinity seemed to wrap around her with suffocating
intensity.

Her heart still thudding unevenly, Alexandra fumbled
with the zip of her skirt. Then she slipped stealthily out of
the room and fled down the stairs. Stuffing her bra and
blouse into her briefcase, she pulled on her jacket and in
guilty turmoil escaped from the house.

The whole way home she marvelled at her stupidity. She
had just sent her whole future up in smoke for the sake of
one night's passion with her ex-husband. I must be mad!
were the words that kept going through her mind as she
drove.

It was just after six o'clock when she arrived home. She made herself a pot of tea and sat down at the kitchen table. The refrigerator's whirr sounded loud in the stillness of the early morning.

The agony of remorse was changing into blazing fury. Last night she'd been ensnared by nostalgia, but doubtless Jim had viewed getting her into bed as nothing more than a challenge. Her self-contempt that she could have slept with him, knowing he was engaged to Juliette, fanned the flames of her white-hot anger.

She was scorched with a sense of shame. With a further twist of anguish she thought of Roxby. She had betrayed him. She couldn't marry him now, although he need never know of her infidelity. To start their life with a lie between them was as unthinkable as confessing to him. Miserably she realised this was the second relationship she had failed with.

It wasn't until she got in to work that Alexandra thought of the law case. Without Roxby's authorisation she couldn't pass it to someone else, and that meant she would have to go on seeing Jim. The prospect filled her with dismay. To have his mocking eyes remind her, as they talked business, that not one detail of her wanton hunger for him had slipped his mind, was more than she could stand. Damn him! She could imagine that he would regard even her embarrassment as just another joke. With his standard of morality, it possibly wouldn't even occur to him that, because of last night, she was going to have to break off her engagement.

Jim had turned her beautifully ordered future into whirling chaos simply to satisfy his ego and to prove he could still have a sexual fling with his ex-wife. Her temper simmered again into a furious resentment. Suddenly she snatched up her phone. Instead of waiting for him to contact her with the taunt of victory in his voice, she was phoning him. She'd let him think she could be as blasé about what had happened as he could.

If she had kept calmer she would have remembered that he would be out of his office that day. It was because of his busy schedule that she had agreed to take the papers to his house in the first place. Thwarted and discouraged, she said there was no message and rang off.

But the need to establish that she was emotionally beyond his reach remained. Taking a steadying breath, she dialled his home number. She cut across him to say a tense hello before realising she was talking to his answering machine. She stared at the receiver in outraged frustration, completely unable to condense what she wanted to say now that she had the opportunity.

If she had needed any confirmation of how little last night had meant to Jim, this was it. He'd left for a meeting with no thought of contacting her over what had happened. It took a second attempt for her to deliver a carefully rehearsed and very casual, 'Hello, Jim. It's Alexandra. I'm phoning to say I think from now on it would be better if we confined our business meetings to my office. Not that last night wasn't wonderful. Physically it was as good as ever, but I'm not going to repeat it.'

Her hand was trembling slightly as she put the phone down. That was one ordeal over. The next would be choosing the right time to tell Roxby, who was coming back from Birmingham today, that she couldn't marry him. Quite what explanation she was going to give him, she hadn't yet worked out. She couldn't dent his pride by admitting she had been unfaithful to him.

Or could she? For a crazy instant she wondered, if she found the courage to confess, if he might somehow manage to forgive her. Realism told her the answer. Her staid fiancé would be shocked speechless by her behaviour. Despondently she reached for some paperwork. It was no use now reminding herself of all his sterling qualities.

It was just before lunch when his secretary came in to tell her that his mother was on the phone. Alexandra guessed something must be wrong for Joyce Robson to call the office long-distance from Devon. Her intuition was right. Roxby's father had collapsed with a heart attack.

Alexandra tried to calm Joyce and to establish how seriously ill William was. Joyce, whose fluting, agitated voice kept breaking, wasn't at all coherent, and the interruption of the pips every few minutes didn't help. She certainly couldn't tell Roxby now that their engagement was off, not with the blow that his father was ill. A wave of compassion hit her, swamping her own turmoil.

The instant he arrived, Alexandra went into his office. The case had gone well and he was in a buoyant mood. It made what she had to say especially hard. She waited for an appropriate pause in his account, and finally, when there wasn't one, she interrupted, 'Darling, listen.' She paused and then said gently, 'I'm afraid I've got bad news for you. Your father's had a heart attack. I don't think he's critical, but your mother wasn't very lucid when she rang from the hospital. She desperately wants you with her.'

'I'll call back immediately,' Roxby said tersely. 'Then I'll have to make plans so I can be out of the office for the next couple of days.'

'Do you want me to come with you?'

'No,' he said abstractedly. 'This is family.'

He kissed her in a perfunctory way and then called his secretary in. Alexandra, who had imagined he'd be glad of her support, looked at him in faint bewilderment. He was already issuing a series of concise instructions to his secretary. It was clear she wasn't needed any longer, so she headed for the door.

'I'll ring you some time this evening, darling,' Roxby said in a preoccupied voice.

'Fine,' she agreed.

Over the next few days he called her regularly at just after six each evening. It turned out that his father's heart attack had been relatively mild, but he was staying on for a short while as his mother didn't want to be on her own. His phone calls left Alexandra feeling thoroughly depressed. She had found a dependable man and she had been too stupid to safeguard their relationship.

She wished Ellen was home. A confidante to talk to would have been comforting. But Ellen wouldn't be back from her holiday till Wednesday night. The only consolation was that she heard nothing from Jim. And even that didn't last long.

She was watching the news on Monday evening when the doorbell rang. With Jingles on her lap it took her a moment to get up. She had tipped the sleepy cat into the armchair and was hunting for her shoes when the bell went again. Not stopping to find them, she went to answer it.

She opened the door to see Jim standing there. Barefooted, she felt even more at a disadvantage with him; he was too tall and too aggressively wide-shouldered. More than that, in jeans and a T-shirt, the pull of his masculinity seemed to threaten her in a way that she didn't want to define. The memory of their lovemaking leapt vividly into prominence and, knowing she was blushing, she began coldly, 'What do you want?'

'First of all to come in,' he said caustically. 'I'm not standing talking to you on the doorstep.'

'You're not coming into my house,' she said emphatically.

For an answer he pushed her into the hall as he strode inside, shutting the door behind him with his foot.

'Just what do you think you're doing?' she demanded,

her voice rising. 'I thought I'd made it clear—I am *not* discussing anything with you outside my office.'

'Although the other night was wonderful and physically we were as good as ever,' he jeered. 'I think that was how you put it.'

'Don't you dare stand there and quote my words at me,' she snapped back. 'You've got a nerve to come here at all!'

'What I've got to say to you isn't the sort of talk for an office setting.'

By now he had propelled her almost to the foot of the stairs. She twisted free from him as he asked, 'Tell me, have you informed Roxby of your little indiscretion?'

'No,' she said, her eyes clashing with his. 'I've taken a leaf out of your book. As it was nothing more than a little indiscretion, there's no need for him to know.'

'But I thought you and Roxby had no secrets,' he taunted.

'You leave Roxby out of this!'

He grabbed hold of her by the wrist.

'Yes, for tonight, why don't we?' he agreed harshly.

'Let go of me!' she gasped as he pulled her with him to the foot of the staircase. 'What the hell do you think you're doing?'

'Leaving Roxby out of it and taking you to bed.'

'You sex-crazed maniac!' she stormed with a mixture of alarm and fury. 'You're not seducing me twice!'

She hit out at him, succeeding in pulling free. She staggered and said angrily, 'Has Juliette become so stingy with her favours that you need to come to me?'

'No, but variety's the spice of life,' he ground back.

He snatched hold of her again, pulling her against his chest. With a muffled gasp she pushed against him, but he only wrapped his arms around her more tightly as he bent his head. A shock of helplessness went through her, and in that moment of vulnerability his lips parted hers, his

mouth exploring hers with a savage demand. Her heart
was hammering so fiercely, she felt almost faint. She
thought the wave that went through her was weakness, not
prepared to admit that its real name was longing.

With her last ounce of strength she began to fight him.
He released her, but not before his mouth had plundered
hers with soul-ravishing intimacy. She caught a glimpse of
his face, dark and relentless and, before she knew what she
was doing, she slapped him with all the force she had.
There was the sharp crack of the blow and then a nerve-
tensing silence. Shaken, she wasn't even aware of how
painfully her hand was smarting.

Her breasts heaved with her ragged breathing as she
glared animosity at him. It was the first time she had seen
him so angry, but she was beyond any sense of caution.

'I'll finish the case for you,' she began, pitching her
voice low in an attempt to keep it steady. 'I'll finish it
because I started it. But once it's over I never want to see
you again.'

Jim rubbed his hand slowly up the side of his face. She
swallowed, curling her fingers into her palms as she forced
herself to meet the glare of anger in his eyes. Bringing his
temper back in check, he ground out, 'I'll be back from
Geneva in a month. In that time, I expect you to have the
case settled.'

In two years of marriage they had never had a scene like
this. Even now that the flash point of their confrontation
was over, the air was full of static electricity. Alexandra
had never heard Jim speak to her with such cold brutality,
and a sharp sense of loss pierced her. With a lift of her
chin she said, 'I suppose Juliette's going to Geneva with
you?'

'Damn right she is,' he answered. 'I want someone
between the sheets with me.'

He strode to the front door and went out. As he

slammed it behind him, she sank down wearily on the bottom stair. Her hand was stinging painfully. She opened her reddened palm, her eyes stormy and her throat tight. Thinking of his parting line, she wished she had hit him even harder.

CHAPTER NINE

ROXBY returned from Devon on Thursday, but Alexandra put off telling him her decision until Saturday evening. She had expected it to be harrowing, and it was. Roxby accepted the diamond ring she handed back to him with the impassive stoicism of a gentleman behaving correctly even in the most difficult of circumstances. His chivalry made her feel so wretched, she could only keep apologising to him.

Needing some commiserative company, the next morning she went next door to see her grandmother.

'Why is it I can't seem to make a permanent relationship with a man?' she asked Ellen bleakly. 'It's got to be my fault, some kind of defect in my character.'

'Don't be silly,' Ellen laughed. 'You and Roxby have got a lifetime ahead of you for a permanent relationship.'

'That's just it—we haven't,' Alexandra sighed. 'Not any more. I've broken off my engagement to him.'

'Well, what brought you to your senses?' Ellen exclaimed, before holding up a placating hand. 'I'm sorry, that was most outspoken of me.'

'I can't believe I've been so stupid,' Alexandra said wearily. 'Roxby was so solid and reliable, and I was too much of a fool to appreciate him.'

'How did he take the news?'

'He took it very well.'

'And that says a lot about your relationship, too,' Ellen observed crisply.

'What do you mean?'

'I mean that when a man is really in love with a woman,

he doesn't take that sort of news very well.'

Alexandra was about to protest when she realised that Ellen had a point. Roxby's initial concern had been the amount of gossip it would cause in the office. It certainly wasn't the reaction of a man who was heartbroken.

'You still haven't said why you've decided not to marry Roxby,' Ellen prompted.

'We . . . we just weren't suited,' Alexandra said evasively.

'It came to you in a flash?' Ellen queried, far too sharp to accept Alexandra's careless explanation.

'No,' she said, before contradicting herself. 'That is, yes. It was a sudden decision. It's all Jim's fault.'

'Jim's?' There was an interested quickness in Ellen's voice. 'How?'

'I had to take some papers round to his house the other evening. We got to talking about the old days . . .' Alexandra broke off and tried again. 'Well, he asked me to stay and have dinner and . . . and I . . .'

She couldn't seem to finish the sentence. She didn't have to. Ellen interrupted her with a meaningful,

'I see. Well, what a blessing you and Jim found out you're still attracted to one another before you made a distastrous marriage.'

'It wouldn't have been a disaster.'

'Of course it would. It couldn't be anything else when you're still in love with your ex-husband.'

'I'm . . .' The denial somehow wouldn't come. The idea brought her up with a jolt. She couldn't possibly be in love with Jim, she thought wildly. Clinging to common sense, she said far more calmly than she felt, 'I'm no more in love with Jim than he is with me.'

'You ridiculous child!' Ellen laughed. 'Of course he's in love with you.'

A crazy thrill of hope went through her. She

immediately despised herself for it. How much evidence
did she need in order to accept reality?

'He's hardly in love with me when he's engaged.'

'What do you mean?' Ellen asked sharply. 'Engaged?'

'Don't sound so surprised,' Alexandra said snappishly.
'*You* were the one who told me.'

'But . . .' Ellen began uncomprehendingly. 'It was
nothing more than a hunch on my part.' She broke off and
then said firmly, 'This is nonsense. Jim can't possibly be
engaged.'

'You've met his fiancée,' Alexandra pointed out wryly.

'You mean . . . that brunette in the restaurant?'

'Yes, Juliette,' Alexandra said stormily.

Ellen drew her brows together in puzzlement, then
exclaimed crossly, 'Oh, I don't understand this at all!'

'You don't understand Jim,' Alexandra told her. 'He
takes love very lightly, as I know only too well.'

She wished she could, too. It was a disheartening
thought that after nearly three years' separation from him
she was still as tied to him emotionally as ever. She didn't
want to admit it, yet how else could she explain the feeling
that was almost relief at being single again? If she couldn't
have Jim in her life, maybe she didn't want anyone.

There were problems at work, too. Roxby avoided her
as much as possible and was extremely curt with her. She
decided it would be better for both of them if she looked
for another job. But she had liked working for the firm
and she knew she'd be sorry to go. She tried to remember
that the lowest ebb signalled the turn of the tide. Surely
things had to get better. They did, but it took her a while
to realise it.

She had at last got a date for the arbitration for Jim's
case. He had been away in Switzerland for a month, and it
was a further week before he made an appointment to see
her. She wasn't looking forward to the meeting. She only

had to think of his comment about wanting Juliette between the sheets with him to feel an upsurge of anger.

She was reading through some correspondence relating to the case when her secretary buzzed her to say that Jim had arrived. The print was blurring and she blinked hard before setting the letter aside. She didn't know if it was overwork or the sultry summer heat, but the last couple of days she had felt very off colour. She wished she felt a bit better. Seeing Jim demanded a hundred per cent strength.

He came into her office and, greeting him calmly, Alexandra indicated the seat opposite her desk. His masculine attractiveness seemed to take her senses a little by surprise. His trip had left him more tanned, making his swarthy looks remind her still more of a buccaneer and setting her heart beating faster than usual.

'Well, how are things?' he began with friendly interest.

He seemed to have forgotten the heated scene between them and the way she'd slapped him. Casually she slipped off her jacket. Small beads of moisture were breaking out on her forehead. She found she was having to concentrate more on suppressing a feeling of queasiness than on what he was saying.

'Do you mind if we get straight down to business?' she asked, cutting him short with an apologetic smile. 'I've got a rather hectic morning.'

Jim gave her a sharp look.

'Sure,' he agreed.

'Well, first of all to bring you up to date——' she said.

She gave him a brief summary of the developments in his absence. She was conscious of his keen, analytic gaze on her.

'Are you OK?' he interrupted. 'You're very pale.'

'I'm fine,' she smiled bravely, contradicting her statement unintentionally by pressing her left hand to her forehead.

'You're not wearing your engagement ring,' he observed immediately.

Alexandra glanced at her hand as though quite surprised herself.

'No,' she agreed simply. She did not want a discussion about her broken engagement.

'So that's why you're looking so wan,' said Jim, studying her. 'Well, am I going to get an explanation of what's happened between you and Roxby?'

'No, you're not,' she said crisply. 'I see I haven't got all the papers here that I need. I won't be a minute.'

She stood up and, as she did so, a wave of sickening giddiness swept over her. With a gasp she clutched at her desk, the room swirling. As swift as a panther, Jim was beside her, his arm going round her waist as she collapsed in a faint.

When she came round a couple of minutes later she was lying on the sofa in Reception. It was the first time she had ever fainted, and she felt frighteningly weary and bewildered. Jim was sitting beside her, rubbing her hand briskly, his dark eyes sharp on her face.

'I . . . I must have fainted,' she said weakly, her voice scarcely sounding like her own.

'You stood up and then just keeled over,' he said, tucking a wisp of silky hair that had come loose from her topknot behind her ear.

The casual tenderness in the gesture made her heart contract. In the time he'd been away she'd done her utmost to convince herself that she wasn't still in love with him. Now those weeks of determination were destroyed in a second.

Her secretary hurried across the reception area, a glass of water in her hand. Jim thanked her as he accepted it and passed it to Alexandra. She took a couple of sips, her strength returning.

'I'm all right now,' she said.

'You'd better lie still for a while,' said Jim, pushing her back as she attempted to sit up. 'I don't want you keeling over again.'

At that moment Roxby came out of the office. He glanced in their direction and then walked over to them. Alexandra took a deep breath. With Jim as an onlooker, she didn't think she could handle Roxby's awkward concern. While Jim explained that she had fainted, she sat up carefully and announced, 'It must have been the heat. I'm fine now.'

'Perhaps when you've recovered fully, you ought to go home,' Roxby suggested curtly. Turning to her secretary, he went on, 'Miss Flynn, would you cancel the rest of Ms Challoner's appointments today?'

Alexandra was about to protest that it was quite unnecessary, and then checked herself. She wasn't going to provoke an argument with Roxby in front of Jim.

'I'm sorry, Jim,' she said. 'I'll make another appointment with you later.'

He grazed a finger down her cheek.

'I'll speak to you again soon.'

There was a purpose in his statement that she didn't like the sound of. He wasn't getting anything out of her concerning her broken engagement. She shied away from his careless touch, her eyes warring with his.

'I can see you're feeling more like your old self already,' he commented, a trace of mockery in his voice.

'I'll be fine as soon as you leave,' she said pointedly, not caring if Roxby did reprimand her afterwards for being rude to a client. The fact that he was her ex-husband would not count as extenuating circumstances.

It was as she was driving home that an uneasy thought occurred to her. Impatiently she dismissed it. Seeing Jim had triggered off the memory of their night together. She reassured herself with the fact that her monthly cycle had always been irregular, and it wasn't new for her to miss a period completely. There was nothing to get alarmed about, she told herself, very alarmed. She'd picked up some sort of virus, that was all. She was certain she couldn't be pregnant.

The pregnancy test she stopped off to buy in a panic at the local chemist indicated that she was wrong. Her visit to her doctor on Saturday morning confirmed the result, and with no difficulty in pinpointing the date of conception he told her she was six weeks pregnant. Although she'd had a couple of days to get used to the idea, Alexandra walked out of the surgery utterly dazed.

She felt she ought to have been aghast. One night's recklessness and she was single and pregnant. Yet suddenly she couldn't stop smiling. She was going to have a baby! Having suppressed her desire for a child for so long, she could scarcely comprehend the dazzling wonder of it. More than that, it was Jim's baby. A sense of joy enveloped her. The future seemed suddenly emblazoned with new meaning.

She felt as if she'd been handed a miracle, a completely unexpected gift, and it was useless to try and be sensible, to think of all the problems of bringing up a child on her own. She was dancing on air. Her need to share the wonderful news with someone sobered her a little. Her mother, still reeling over the disappointment that Alex was no longer engaged to Roxby, was hardly going to stand up to knowing that she was now pregnant by Jim. How she was going to break it to her she didn't know, but for the moment she was too elated to be worried.

She couldn't stop making plans. She would have to be a working mother, of course, but that wouldn't stop her from providing her baby with the most loving of homes. She reluctantly conceded that it would have been better to be having a child within the stability of marriage and, for a wistful moment, she wondered if Jim might have stayed faithful to her if she'd conceived in the time they had been together.

Firmly she put the idea out of her mind. He was going to marry Juliette, and that was an end to it. Furthermore, he wasn't even going to know she was having his baby. If he did, she'd never get him out of her life. She couldn't endure having him visit her when he was married to Juliette. The only thing for it was a clean break.

Although she was brimming with excitement, there was no one, apart from her grandmother, she felt ready to tell. She thought Ellen would understand her delight, yet just the same she felt a shade hesitant about dropping such a bombshell. Confessing that at a worldly-wise twenty-nine she had accidentally got pregnant in a night of passion wasn't going to be easy.

She asked Ellen to have lunch with her, waited for what she thought was a suitable moment, and then said boldly, deciding on the direct approach, 'Gran, I've got something to tell you. You'd better brace yourself for this one, because it's going to come as a bit of a shock.' She paused, and then announced, 'I'm going to have a baby.'

Ellen stared at her and quickly set her coffee-cup down on the table.

'Well,' she said breathlessly, 'you're right—this is a surprise! Surprise, mind—I'm not shocked. I . . . er . . . take it Jim's the father?'

Alexandra nodded and then admitted with a small breath of laughter, 'This is a relief. I wasn't quite sure how you'd react.'

'Oh, this sort of thing happened even in my day,' Ellen said, before adding with a sigh, 'Besides, I feel I'm partly to blame. After all, I was matchmaking between the two of you as hard as I could.'

'I thought I was right to suspect you!'

'You don't sound very dismayed,' Ellen said questioningly.

'Dismayed?' Alexandra laughed. 'I'm over the moon!'

Ellen smiled and said, 'I never did believe all that talk of yours about not wanting children.'

'I was resigned to what I felt was the inevitable,' Alexandra admitted. 'There seemed to be no point in hankering after what I couldn't have. But now that I've found out I'm pregnant, it's the most wonderful thing that's ever happened to me.'

'Have you told Jim yet?'

'No. And I'm not going to,' Alexandra said positively. 'This is *my* baby. It has nothing to do with Jim.'

'As the father, he has a right to know,' Ellen replied firmly. 'And, added to that, it could change everything.'

'I'm not getting married just because I'm having a baby. That's even if Jim was to ask me. But he happens to be engaged. No, the way I see it, this baby is completely mine, and you're not to breathe a word of it to him. I want your promise.'

'How can I possibly make a promise like that?'

'Because I'm asking you to. Jim and I are never going to get back together. It'll be best all round if he never knows.'

'Well, he'll find out sooner or later,' Ellen said.

'No, he won't, because I've thought of that. I've already worked out what I'm going to do. First of all I'm going to hand in my notice at work. I'll have to find another job to support me and the baby, but that can wait for a while, and I've put Roxby through enough without carrying on at the office visibly pregnant. Then I'm going to put this house on the market and look for somewhere to live in Gloucester.'

'Gloucester? Well, I can't see any sense in that at all,' said Ellen. 'Really, Alexandra, hasn't it occurred to you that as a single parent you're going to need all the help you can get? Bringing up a child is hard work.'

'I know it is,' Alexandra agreed. 'But there's no way I'm staying here so that Jim will find out I'm having his baby.'

'You're stubborn at times,' Ellen said disapprovingly, before stating purposefully, 'I suppose the only thing for it, then, is that I shall have to move too.'

'You mean you'd sell up and come and live near me?'

'You don't think I'm going to miss out on my first great grandchild, do you?'

Alexandra hugged her gratefully.

'Gran, you're wonderful!' she exclaimed.

An ally was going to make everything so much easier. Having worked out her strategy, first thing on Monday morning she went into Roxby's office to tell him that she would be resigning. He greeted the news with visible relief, so much so that instead of having a month to work out he arranged that she could leave that Friday.

He dismissed her concern that it would mean leaving several cases outstanding, including Jim's. He assured her it would be no problem and that he would take over the Global Freightways case himself.

In many ways she was quite glad to be taking a break from work. She was suffering badly from morning sickness. Preoccupied with nausea, she found it hard to tackle her workload with her usual energy and drive. Ellen was sympathetic.

'I remember I was just the same when I was expecting Olivia,' she said. 'But it passes. In a few weeks you'll go to bed one evening and realise suddenly that you haven't felt queasy all day.'

That, and her elation at being pregnant, kept Alexandra's spirits up.

She was feeling particularly fragile when Ellen called in

to see her at the weekend. Sitting listlessly on the sofa, she was certain that to move would be disastrous.

'Have you had breakfast?' asked Ellen.

'Don't mention food,' Alexandra moaned. 'I haven't even managed to feed the cat yet!'

'Well, that's something I can see to. And then I'll make you a nice pot of tea and some dry toast for you to nibble.'

Ellen bustled through into the kitchen while Alexandra, determined that it was all a matter of mental control, picked up the newspaper. It didn't help much. Ellen had just set a tray down beside her when a car drew up outside. Glancing out of the window, she announced, pleased, 'Here's Jim!'

'Oh, no!' Alexandra groaned. 'What on earth can he want?'

'To see you, I expect,' Ellen said drily.

She went to let him in, giving Alexandra no time to retaliate. Hearing their voices in the hall, Alexandra made a supreme effort to rally. At least she was tidily dressed in cotton slacks and top. Her hair wasn't in its usual smooth chignon, but she had tied it back. Thank goodness she'd resisted the temptation to get up in her dressing-gown.

As he came into the room she managed to say quite brightly, 'Hello, Jim. This is a surprise.'

'I thought I'd call in to see how you're feeling. I was worried about you the other day.'

He waited till Ellen was seated, and then sat down on the sofa. Alexandra wished he'd chosen the armchair opposite. He unsettled her, and she wasn't feeling strong enough to cope with any emotional turmoil. With stoic cheerfulness she said, 'Oh, I'm quite recovered now.'

His eyes went to the tray on the table beside her. She might have guessed he was too sharp to miss that she was getting the invalid treatment from Ellen.

'Sure?' he asked, his dark eyes meeting hers.

'Yes, there's nothing wrong with Alexandra,' Ellen put in brightly. 'She's not ill.'

She managed to put the stress very nicely on the last word, and Alexandra gave her a quick glare of reproach. Ellen had given her solemn word over this.

Her grandmother hurriedly avoided her gaze and asked Jim about his trip. Alexandra was glad not to have to participate too much in the conversation. Her main concern was how she could push the tray further away from her so she wouldn't have to smell the toast.

'Well,' said Ellen, 'I mustn't sit here any longer. I only popped in for a few moments, and I've got some shopping to do.'

Alexandra was about to get up and see her out, but Ellen stopped her.

'No, dear, you stay where you are. And do try to eat a little something.'

She went out of the room. Hearing the front door click, Alexandra said, desperate for a diversion, 'I've been meaning to contact you, Jim. I wanted to tell you that Roxby's going to be handling the case from now on.'

'I thought you said you were feeling OK?' Jim queried, as though her information had made no impact.

'I am,' she lied, clenching her hands.

He reached out and took hold of her by the arm. The concern in his eyes was too much for her.

'Oh, hell!' she exclaimed weakly.

Clamping her hand over her mouth, she stood up and rushed into the kitchen. She was bowed over the sink, clutching at the rim, her fight against nausea lost, when Jim came in.

'Go away,' she whispered despairingly, totally humiliated.

Instead he held her shoulders while she retched helplessly. When the spell had passed she sagged against him, weak with mortification. He pushed her gently on to one of the kitchen chairs.

'Will you please go away?' she whispered, very close to tears.

He ran his handkerchief under the tap and pressed it on her forehead. The coolness was wonderful.

'Have you been to the doctor?' he asked impatiently.

'Yes, of course I've been to the doctor,' she snapped back.

She raised anxious eyes to his, realising that her reply and the tone of it were incautious. In that moment, she saw comprehension darken his face.

'Good lord!' he exclaimed with muted fury. 'That bastard's got you pregnant! I'm right, aren't I?'

His savage voice on top of the humiliation of being sick in front of him made her courage break without warning. Suddenly she burst into tears. Drawing up a chair, Jim sat down beside her, pulling her close while she sobbed incoherently, 'Don't you . . . call Roxby a bastard! I . . . wanted to marry him. I would have done if . . .' Her voice broke and she couldn't go on.

She could sense Jim's anger even in the protective way he was holding her, but she was too distraught to make any sense of it. Giving up her attempts to establish her independence, she wept, turning her face into his shoulder. It took her a while to steady. Strangely, Jim, who was good at being comforting, didn't murmur any soothing words.

With a little convulsive catch of breath, Alexandra drew away from him. Smoothing her hair, she tried to recover a remnant of dignity.

'I'm sorry,' she said in a strangled voice. 'I didn't mean to break down in front of you.'

'What are you going to do?' Jim's voice was quiet and oddly harsh.

'What do you mean, what am I going to do?' she asked, steeling herself to glance at him.

'I mean,' he said, a shade caustically, 'are you going to have the baby?'

She stared at him in outrage. For a moment she was almost robbed of speech, and then indignation brought back her fighting spirit with a rush.

'Of course I'm going to have the baby,' she told him heatedly. 'And don't you *dare* suggest anything else!'

'OK,' he said, anger in his voice, 'simmer down. I wasn't to know you held such trenchant opinions on the subject.'

'Well, you know now. I happen to want this baby. I've waited for it almost all my life. It's going to be one of the most wanted babies that's ever been born!'

She saw from the tightness of his cheek muscles that he was still having difficulty in mastering his temper. It gave her the courage to say, 'It's sweet of you to be concerned about me, but really, I'm going to manage fine.'

'Why did Roxby break off your engagement?'

The suddenness of the question and the way it was fired at her took her by surprise.

'He didn't break it off. *I* did.'

'Come on, Alex,' said Jim impatiently as he stood up, 'don't give me that. I know you've got your pride, but I want the truth out of you.'

'You've got the truth,' she said, trailing off a little towards the end because it certainly wasn't the whole and absolute truth. 'Look, I don't want to talk about this any more,' she said in a cramped voice.

Hands in the pockets of his jeans, Jim paced about the kitchen. Alexandra was only just beginning to appreciate what a narrow escape she'd had, with him jumping to the conclusion that the baby was Roxby's.

'Well,' he commented harshly, 'you never know

anyone, do you?'

She wasn't quite sure what he meant by that. She could only think he was surprised that she had come to terms so easily with being an unmarried mother. His next comment suggested her assumption was right.

'What does Olivia make of all this?'

'She . . . um . . . she's furious with me. At the moment she's not talking to me. I'll just have to hope she'll get used to the idea with a bit more time.'

Jim swore under his breath. He was pacing about her small kitchen with the leashed energy of something wild, dangerous and caged.

'Jim, honestly,' she insisted, 'I'm going to be fine. Don't worry about me. Anyway, it has nothing to do with you.'

He stared at her, his gaze uncomfortably piercing. There was a long pause and then he said, 'You take good care of yourself.' His voice softened a little as, bending to brush her cheek with his lips, he added, 'I'll see you some time.'

He strode out of the room and, her heart contracting a little, Alexandra propped an elbow on the kitchen table. His last remark had sounded very much like a goodbye. She shook her regrets off, forcing herself to be sensible. Everything had worked out for the best, even though she hadn't had a hand in it.

It had never occurred to her that Jim would automatically assume Roxby was the father of her baby. Even if she had wanted to, he'd scarcely given her the chance to deny it. This altered her plans. With Jim believing Roxby was the father, she didn't need to escape to Gloucester any more. Ellen had been valiant in saying she would uproot herself again, but at her age it wasn't really fair to expect it of her. Now they could both stay where they were.

She was aware of a faint stab of conscience at keeping

the truth from Jim. Then she dismissed it. He was engaged to Juliette. Even if she told him and he gallantly asked her to marry him, she would refuse. He didn't love her, so it wouldn't work and it wouldn't last, any more than it had the last time, and she was determined that her baby was going to have a stable home. She was fighting for emotional survival here, and that meant she couldn't afford to weaken. Jim was never going to know.

CHAPTER TEN

IT WAS six o'clock on Monday evening and Alexandra had gone out into the front garden to stake some gladioli. She hadn't been working long when Jim's car drew up outside. She was surprised to see him, but she smiled and laid the ball of twine aside. Then, seeing the forceful energy with which Jim got out of the driving seat and came towards her, she got rather defensively to her feet.

He strode up to her, his face set in determined lines. With his powerful physique and swift movements, he was somewhat overpowering, but she didn't get the chance to ask him what was wrong. Catching hold of her by the elbow, he marched her towards the house.

'You and I are going to talk,' he began ominously.

'Talk? What about?' she began, starting to protest.

'I suggest you come quietly. If not, the neighbours are going to have a field day,' he replied grimly.

He marshalled her into the house, not letting go of her until they were in the sitting-room.

'Jim, what is this all about?' she demanded heatedly as she pulled away from him.

'I'll tell you,' he said, his voice lightly sarcastic. 'I've just been to see your ex-fiancé.'

Alexandra's startled eyes looked up into his.

'Oh, no,' she said faintly.

'Oh, yes,' he mocked.

She thought she'd better sit down. She hesitated a moment, and then asked tentatively, afraid of the answer, 'What . . . what did you say to him?'

'Well, considering I thought he'd broken off your

engagement, got you pregnant and given you the sack, what do you think I said to him?'

Aghast, Alexandra took a second to ask, 'You . . . you didn't hurt him, did you?'

'You needn't worry—Roxby's still in one piece. Luckily, despite the smooth manner, he's quite a fast talker when it comes to the crunch. He gave me a lot of facts very quickly. One being that he wasn't the one who broke off your engagement . . .'

'*I'd* told you that,' she interrupted, recovered enough now to retaliate.

'But you omitted the second. Not only is the baby not Roxby's, but it turns out you'd never even been to bed with him.'

She got swiftly to her feet in one furious movement.

'How dare you discuss my sex life with him?'

'And how dare *you* tell me you're carrying Roxby's baby when the child's mine?'

She glared at him. There was a brief taut silence, and then she said coolly, and with a slight lift of her chin, 'You're making rather an assumption, aren't you?'

The gleam in his eyes warned her, but it was too late to shy away. He snatched hold of her, pulling her fiercely to his chest by her forearms.

'There are times when I could shake you!' he exploded. 'Considering you weren't even sleeping with your fiancè, it's hardly likely you were in the sack with anyone else, now is it? The child's mine, and you damn well know it!'

'Do you have to express yourself so crudely?' she flared.

'I'm not concerned with the finer points of English,' Jim fired back. 'I'm concerned with the question of paternity.'

'All right,' she conceded, struggling to free herself, 'the baby's yours.'

'And when were you planning to tell me this amazing

piece of news?' he asked as he released her.

'I wasn't,' she said defiantly.

'No,' he agreed sarcastically, 'you were going to let me go on thinking it was Roxby's. If I hadn't gone to see him today to tell him I didn't appreciate his treatment of my ex-wife and he'd better do the right thing and marry you, I'd still be in the dark.'

'You . . . you told him he'd got to marry me?'

'Yes. I called him a cad—you remember that quaint, old-fashioned word you called me not so long back?'

Alexandra wanted to be furious with him for dragging Roxby into this, but instead the thought of him going immediately to her defence was singularly touching. She was about to tell him she appreciated it when he went on, 'So, in view of the fact that we've now established that the child's mine, it might be an idea if we get some plans sorted out.'

'Plans?' she repeated warily. 'I've already made my plans. This is *my* baby, Jim. And you're not having anything to do with it.'

'Like hell I'm not!'

'You're not complicating my life any more,' she said with equal vehemence. 'I'm perfectly capable of bringing up a child on my own, and I don't need your help.'

She wasn't having him walking in when Juliette would allow it to bring her baby some expensive present. Firmly she went on, 'I'm fortunate that financially I can go it alone. What the baby lacks in luxuries will be more than compensated for by love. So you needn't think you're breezing in to see my child when it suits you and undoubtedly assuming you can get me in the sack, as you so crudely put it, at the same time.'

'And you're not cheating me of my son——'

'So you've already decided it's a son!' she broke in angrily. 'Do I take it that if it's a daughter you won't feel quite so cheated?'

'You can cut the courtroom tactics with me,' snapped Jim. 'And if you'd let me finish a sentence, you'd know I don't mind what sex the child is. This baby happens to be precious.'

'It wasn't so precious to you a few days ago when you asked me if I intended having it,' she reminded him, her stormy eyes clashing with his.

'I didn't know it was mine then,' he pointed out with rapidly diminishing patience. 'I was concerned for you having a baby I thought you didn't want.'

'Well, now I've put you right on that. It's going to be the most wanted baby——' she began.

'I can endorse that point,' he cut across her. He took a step nearer and she willed herself to hold her ground. 'And let me add another. There is no way on earth that you're doing me out of what's mine—I'm going to see to that.'

'Are you?' she replied. 'And how exactly do you intend doing it?'

His gaze held hers for an instant. She was aware of the hard brilliance of his dark eyes, of the angry, determined set of his jaw. Not even three years' separation had diminished the attraction he had for her. She could do nothing about the thudding of her heart as their eyes met. It was a reflex action.

'I'm going to marry you,' said Jim with quiet ferocity.

Alexandra was so taken aback that she wasn't ready with a scathing reply. Then, finding her voice, she managed, 'Oh, no, you're not! The only reason that you're asking me to marry you is that you want my baby. Well, you don't win like that. And, furthermore,' she continued, anger strengthening her tone, 'you seem to have forgotten that Juliette happens to be involved in this.'

'I've told Juliette you're pregnant.'

'Have you? Well, between us we really have messed

things up nicely for all concerned. I suppose she's released you from your promise to her. Well, thank you very much, but such a noble sacrifice from the two of you won't be necessary.'

'Woman, you are impossible!' roared Jim with sudden fury. 'I've never met anyone who can be as thoroughly irrational as you can!'

Alexandra was so outraged by his proposal it didn't occur to her to be intimidated by his pent-up rage. As he snatched hold of her she stormed, 'Then you'll be very relieved to know you won't have to put up with me. I wouldn't have you as a gift on a silver platter! I'm not marrying you—once was enough! You haven't got a clue what marriage is about. I suppose you think you'll have me sitting at home with the baby while you're off free to carry on exactly as before!'

Jim's strong fingers bit into her arm as he gripped her hard. His eyes glittered as he cut across her.

'In three years you haven't changed one bit, have you? As always, you're obsessed with your career.'

'At least it never let me down the way you did. With such different values, we couldn't expect to have a marriage that lasted,' she retaliated.

'But you weren't pregnant then. Now you are. So you needn't think this is the end of it.'

He released her so abruptly that she almost staggered, and he strode out of the room. A second later she heard the front door slam behind him. She swept into the kitchen and filled the kettle. She needed a cup of tea to calm her down.

It was some while later, and she was curled up on the sofa with a magazine, when the phone rang. She went to answer it. If that was Jim, she still had plenty more to say to him. Prepared for a continuation of hostilities, she was brought up with quite a jolt when she heard her mother's lyrical voice.

'I thought you weren't speaking to me,' she spluttered.

'That was just shock,' Olivia replied serenely. 'You must admit, it was a lot to adjust to. But I've always prided myself on being very resilient.'

Alexandra repressed a smile and said immediately, 'Well, it's nice to hear from you.'

'The reason I'm calling is that I want to arrange a shopping expedition.'

'What do we want a shopping expedition for?'

'Because my grandchild is going to have the best,' Olivia replied. 'Harrods has a very good baby department. We'll decide on the nursery together. Really, Alexandra, I was beginning to think I'd never be a grandmother. I'm quite excited!'

Alexandra, glad that her mother had accepted the idea that she would be a single parent, listened tactfully while Olivia enthused about the excellent gynaecologist she knew and the latest line of thought on natural childbirth. This was not the moment to antagonise her by insisting on her independence. Gradually she would establish that she had her own ideas where the baby was concerned.

They chatted for a while, and then Alexandra asked, 'Mother, do you think I'm being unreasonable in wanting to bring this baby up on my own?'

'I didn't think you had any choice, dear,' Olivia said with a wealth of meaning.

'Well, I have. Jim's expressed a great interest in the baby.'

'But not enough interest to marry you,' her mother said disapprovingly.

'Oh, yes, he has,' said Alexandra, defending him.

There was an instant's silence and then Olivia cooed, 'Darling, this is wonderful! Why didn't you tell me straight away? I must start planning for the w——'

'Mother,' Alexandra cut across her, 'I said Jim had asked me. I didn't say I'd said yes.'

'Oh, but you will, pet. Of course you're keeping him guessing; any woman would. But now everything's going to be fine. And I'll make all the arrangements for the wedding.'

'We'll talk about this later,' said Alexandra, in despair of making her mother understand, and wishing she'd never been rash enough to admit so much. 'I'll put you in the picture when I see you on Thursday.'

She was not entering into a marriage of convenience to suit Jim and her mother. But the pressure was getting a bit much from all sides, and it was certain to intensify. She had always been able to stand up to Olivia's bulldozing, but Ellen's subtle persuasiveness called for more resilience. She was beginning to feel she could do with a holiday to get away from it all.

The idea had considerable appeal. When her divorce from Jim had been finalised she had spent a week in North Wales at a hotel not far from Dolgellau, overlooking the Mawddach estuary. With its welcoming atmosphere it had been a comfortable and peaceful haven. Now she was at another crossroads in her life when she needed to make plans and to find an inner core of strength. She decided she would phone the next day and book up a short holiday.

The hotel was able to offer her accommodation for the following weekend. Having got the holiday settled, she debated calling Jim. She had spent a restless night thinking about him. Although he had provoked her beyond measure, she was regretting having been so fiery-tempered.

She had no intention of accepting his pragmatic proposal but, now that she was calmer, she knew that when it came to it she couldn't deprive him completely of his child. Of course he had been angry with her. And, what was more, a child needed a father figure. Alexandra knew what it was like to grow up with no father in the background. She wanted better than that for her baby. But marrying him because she was pregnant, with Juliette still somewhere in the equation, was out of the question.

She rang his number at work and was quickly put through to him. Resolutely she began, 'Hello, Jim. It's Alex.'

She didn't even notice that unthinkingly she had slipped back into using the pet name he had always called her.

'Well, this is unexpected! I thought you had some rather strong feelings where I'm concerned. Or did I only get that impression because you turned down flat my offer of marriage?'

'I over-reacted,' she admitted coolly. 'Not that I've changed my mind about marrying you, but I've phoned to apologise for my behaviour.'

'That's big of you!'

Her eyes darkened a little, but she still refused to be goaded by the dry note in his voice.

'All right,' she said, 'I should have told you about the baby.'

There was a pause, then Jim said, 'And I shouldn't have shouted at you.'

His answer mollified her. Choosing her words carefully, she went on, 'I've been thinking about the baby, and what I said was wrong. Every child has the right to know both its parents, so I've decided to let you take on the responsibilities of a father. But that doesn't mean *I* want anything to do with you.'

'If this baby's going to grow up with a gulf of hostility between us, having two parents isn't going to do him a lot of good,' Jim commented. 'Still, I accept your apology. I realise that for someone of your temperament it can't have been easy to make the call.'

Alexandra thought she would explode at his infernal cheek!

'You can leave my temperament out of it,' she told him shortly. 'In view of your role in all this, I think I'm being both practical and extremely generous.'

'You are indeed,' he said drily. 'You'll endure me for the sake of our child. Well, it's a start. How about having dinner with me on Saturday evening to celebrate the end of the cold war?'

Somehow he seemed to have snatched the initiative from her. She had been about to suggest that they needed to talk so that they could establish the basis for their future relationship. With no logical reason not to accept, she said, keeping her voice cool and businesslike, 'That's fine. Shall we say seven-thirty?'

'See you then.'

She found that in some curious way she was looking forward to having dinner with him. And this time, confident that she was handling the situation with the same sound judgement she'd always applied to her work, she felt quite buoyant. Only occasionally did wistfulness catch at her. She refused to give in to it. Jim would always be too much of a womaniser to provide the sort of relationship based on lifelong trust and commitment that she craved.

She changed into a pretty block print dress that had a matching blouson-style jacket. Jingles, who was sitting in the middle of her duvet, blinked at her before curling up contentedly. She sat down on the bed and reached out to stroke him before fastening the straps of her cream sandals.

She had deliberately chosen high-heeled shoes. Soon she would have to adjust to flatter ones as her balance changed with the baby, and with Jim, unlike Roxby, however high her heels, she would still only reach his shoulder.

She reached for her atomiser of Rive Gauche, and then

changed her mind and decided on Femme instead, for tonight she felt a woman in all its many meanings: mature, fulfilled and independent. She could cope with Jim. At long last she seemed to have acquired some common sense where he was concerned. She and the baby would be a complete family unit with him there in the background, but only out of the kindness of her heart.

She heard his car pull up outside, and smiled in spite of herself. She checked the impulse to run downstairs and let him in before he rang. She might be in control of the situation, but it was only prudent to remind herself that Jim had a lot of sexual charisma and she had to tread warily.

When she opened the door to him, his masculine attractiveness made her realise how right she was. In a suit with a Givenchy shirt his urbanity was unsettling. Alexandra felt the magnetism of his tough, virile appeal, and knew she would have to be very careful this evening.

He was holding a bouquet of pink roses and carnations that were in a cloud of gypsophila. As she invited him in, he handed the flowers to her.

'They're beautiful, Jim,' she said, hoping he wouldn't notice that her voice was a little husky. She had chosen these same flowers to carry in a spray that day, five years ago, when they were married.

'Beautiful flowers for a beautiful lady,' he commented, adding with a trace of speculation, 'Beautiful and a little sad?'

'Not me,' she denied quickly. 'Why should I be sad? Do you want to think I'm lonely without you? Sorry to disillusion you, Jim, but I'm not.'

'I thought we'd decided we weren't fighting tonight,' he said, mocking her tone.

She put the flowers in a large vase. Arranging them would be something for tomorrow, a kind of lengthening of the pleasure of being with him. She caught herself quickly. This was no time for sentimentality.

Rather briskly she changed the topic of conversation. Establishing the right note was important. She was concentrating so hard on it that at first she took no notice of the route Jim was taking them. It was with a little jolt of surprise that she realised he was turning into the car park of the Casa Alta, a restaurant that had been a favourite of hers when they were married. She hadn't been back since they'd been divorced, and his choice, together with the flowers, made her start to suspect him. If he thought he could sweet-talk her into anything he was going to be disappointed!

'What are you looking at me so warily for?' asked Jim as he pulled into a parking space. 'You always used to like an evening here. And the guitar music is even better now than it was then, if that's possible.'

'It may be, but our last trip down memory lane has warned me off nostalgia.'

'Quite a trip, though, wasn't it?'

Alexandra realised to her annoyance that she was colouring slightly. She should have been more careful with her choice of words. It hurt her to think that he'd been back to the restaurant since they had divorced. She couldn't have come here with another man—it belonged too much to them. Such a thought had obviously never occurred to Jim. Why did she always make the mistake of assuming he shared her regrets about their break-up? If he had, he would never have let her go so easily.

The Casa Alta was always crowded on a Saturday night. Jim must have booked a table, for the head waiter came up immediately to ask them if they would like an aperitif and to show them to their table. It was set aside in a little alcove. The restaurant had a rustic charm with its solid wooden banquettes and rough white walls that were hung with flowers in pretty little ceramic pots. In the main part of the dining-room at the end of the small dance-floor, two guitarists were playing. Alexandra turned her head and watched them while Jim ordered.

'I think I've chosen a carefully nutritious meal for you,' he said as the waiter moved away.

'I've always eaten the right foods,' she smiled, responding in spite of herself to the banter in his voice and teasing him in return. 'And I don't think the part of the worried father suits you.'

'You wait till the great day,' he said. 'I'll beat all the other men at pacing up and down the hospital corridor.'

'That's facetious!'

'It's meant to be. I'm planning on being with you for the birth.'

Surprised, she raised her eyes to his. They were shrewd, quizzical, and with a caressing warmth she knew far better than to trust.

'You can think again on that one,' she told him.

'You don't want me to hold your hand?'

She realised she would like it very much, but it wasn't going to happen. She had to be emotionally independent of him.

'We'll discuss it nearer the time,' she said hurriedly. 'We've got other things to sort out right now.'

'OK, let's deal with them. I take it you've come to a decision about what part you're going to let me play in all this?'

'That's right, I have.'

It should have occurred to her that he was being far too amenable, but it didn't.

'I admit,' she went on, 'there will be some things we'll need to decide together. I'm prepared to let you have your say in things like schools and so on . . .'

'So I can be of use in about five years' time,' he said

sarcastically. 'Well, that's great. I was hoping to establish some sort of relationship with our child a little earlier than that.'

'You're deliberately raising difficulties,' she told him shortly.

'No, I'm listening with interest to your proposals.'

'Which you haven't got much option but to accept,' she reminded him pointedly. 'I was thinking of you visiting us, say, the first Sunday of every month, but I'm not having you dropping in as and when you feel like it.'

Jim's serious nod seemed to indicate his agreement. He seemed quite prepared to let the matter drop now that it was settled, and moved the conversation to more general topics. Alexandra reflected how amazingly simple it had been to get her own way, despite his forceful personality, just by being calm and quietly determined.

The guitars' rhythm changed to a fast, restless clip. Jim tapped his fingers lightly on the table in time to it. She noted their long gracefulness, the strength in his wristbones and the gold Piaget watch against his tanned skin. He had strong hands, hands that could cherish and protect. The music in the bass strings throbbed with a restlessness and passion. She fought to bring her emotions under control.

'Has gypsy music lost its appeal for you?' queried Jim.

The word gypsy reminded her instantly of Juliette. She wondered if they had broken up with a violent row, with Juliette throwing his ring back at him. It seemed highly likely, considering the circumstances. But she couldn't guess from Jim's behaviour with her what his feelings were about it. She would never understood him where women were concerned, and she certainly wasn't going to ask him about his ex-fiancèe.

'No, the music doesn't have quite the appeal for me it once did,' she answered.

'You mean you've suppressed the gypsy in you at last?'

'There never was a gypsy in me,' she replied, her eyes clashing with his.

'You're wrong about that,' he answered. 'You always were very free-spirited. I stupidly thought that if I gave you enough freedom we'd make a go of it together.'

'I think you were the one who enjoyed freedom within our marriage,' she retorted, her eyes becoming stormy.

'I don't follow you,' he said, his gaze narrowing on her.

'It's not important,' Alexandra said quickly.

It was the only flare-up of the evening. They lingered over coffee, but she said she didn't want to dance. The spell of the music was too strong, and it would only make her sad. Jim suggested that they leave and, a little sorry that the evening was over, she agreed.

She assumed he intended driving her straight home, but instead she found that they were heading in the opposite direction, towards Rickmansworth.

'Jim, what is this?' she demanded. 'I thought you were taking me home.'

'I am. But not till after we've talked,' he answered calmly.

'Talked? We've spent the whole evening talking!'

'You've spent the whole evening talking nonsense. I thought I'd let you plough steadily on till you ran out of steam. I always did go for that cool, crisp lawyer manner you put on at times. But now we're alone together you can drop it and we'll talk sense.'

'You . . .' she began. 'Do you mean . . .?'

'I mean I've got no intention of seeing you just once a month and then solely because of the baby.'

Alexandra realised he had sat opposite her all evening blandly appearing to agree with her when he'd been intending this manoeuvre all along. She couldn't begin to express her annoyance, which was directed half at him and half at herself for being so self-congratulatory, when she should have known better than to underestimate her opponent.

'You turn this car round and take me home,' she demanded. 'I might have guessed if I gave you an inch you'd take five miles!'

'Now *I've* paid you the courtesy of listening to *you*,' said Jim, slanting her a glance, 'I think you could at least do the same for me.'

'I can't think you could have anything to say that I could possibly be interested in,' she retorted, cool anger in her voice to conceal her slight apprehension.

'Well, you always could be obtuse at times when it suited you,' he observed.

'Have you finished insulting my intelligence?' she flashed back with the icy retaliatory comment of the loser.

He turned into his drive and walked round to open her door for her. Having escorted her inside, he offered her a liqueur. She promptly turned it down, but, not the least discomfited by her frostiness, Jim put some classical guitar music on the stereo.

'If you think you can get round me with some sentimental music, a drink and your undoubted charm, Jim,' she warned, 'I'm afraid you're going to be disappointed.'

'Give me credit for being a little more subtle than that,' he said drily, adding, 'I've tried shouting at you. This time I thought I'd make an appeal to calm reason and hope I get a better response.'

'As I assume you intend keeping me here until you've said whatever you're going to, I suppose you'd better get it over with,' she said.

'Might I suggest you sit down?' he said with light sarcasm. 'And it would be nice if you could listen to this with an open mind.'

'I know far too much about you for that,' she retorted as she sat down on the edge of an armchair.

'I don't think you know very much about men at all, but at the moment, that, and the influence your father's had on you, isn't the issue.'

'What on earth are we talking about my father for? I haven't seen him since I was about ten!'

'And isn't that what you're afraid of? That I'll desert your baby the way he deserted you?'

The remark was far too close to the truth. Alexandra hated the way Jim could pick up on her thought-waves before she'd consciously sorted them out herself. It made her say scathingly, 'Is the psychoanalysis over for this evening, or is there more to come?'

'There's more,' he said. He sat down on the sofa, drawing his hawkish brows together as he went on, 'No matter what you think, I'm never going to let this child of ours down the way your father let you down.'

'Is that the whole of what you have to say to me?' she demanded, antagonism in her voice.

'No,' he said forcefully. 'The rest of it is that I still think we should get married. You're having a baby, and the best way to give it the upbringing we both want for it is by us getting married.'

'Fine,' she said crisply. 'That's the calm, logical persuasion bit over, is it? Because if so, the answer's still the same. It's no, just as it always will be. I may be a fool at times, but I don't repeat my mistakes twice.'

She stood up, and as she did so Jim leapt to his feet.

'Now you listen . . .' he began as he grabbed hold of her.

'You let go of me!'

'Not till I get some sense out of you.'

'You mean not till I give in,' she corrected him heatedly. 'Do you really think I'm going to marry you for no better reason than the fact that you've decided it would be nice to have a son?'

'I thought I'd already made it clear I'd be pleased with a girl or a boy,' said Jim. 'But now you come to mention it, a son would have its appeal. The idea of a daughter who might turn out to be as volatile as her mother is a bit much, even for me!'

Alexandra laughed angrily as she replied, 'The rate we're going, we'd have a wonderful marriage, wouldn't we? Lately we've done nothing but fight.'

'Lately we've started to communicate. Physically we were always made for each other. And whatever our disagreements, at least we know how to make up.'

The tone of his voice didn't warn her of his intention. Cupping her face with determined hands, he bent his head to kiss her. Unprepared, she could do nothing about the helpless shock of response that went through her. For a second all the stubborn resistance went out of her at the feel of his mouth, sensuous and demanding on hers. Then sanity took over and, her heart racing, she turned her head away from his kiss.

'How typical!' she stormed, knowing he must have sensed the tremor of desire that had gone through her at his touch. 'All that talk about logic and reasoning, and when it comes down to it all you're concerned with is sex!'

'We can't all be as high-minded as you and Roxby,' he mocked harshly as, catching hold of her wrists so she couldn't hit out at him, he kissed her again.

Held prisoner by him, she couldn't break free. His mouth found hers again in a hard, searching kiss that demanded a response. She refused to give it, despite the wild flicker of pleasure that danced along her nerves.

When finally Jim raised his head to give her a quizzical look, she said breathlessly, her face flushed, 'Nothing you can say is going to get me to marry you, any more than this is.'

'You mean you're not attracted to me any more.'

'That's right,' she lied emphatically.

'OK, if that's the way you want to have it——' he agreed as he started to take the pins out of her hair.

'What do you think you're doing?' she demanded, her hand going to her chignon that was already tumbling loose.

'Giving you the chance to show me you're not turned on by me any more,' he said, a predatory gleam of challenge in his eyes as his gaze held hers for an instant before travelling to her lips.

Her breath seemed to have locked in her throat, otherwise she would have come back with a short answer. Jim bent his head slowly to kiss her again with a sensuous but persistent patience, his hand sliding up between her shoulder-blades, pressing her breasts against the hard strength of his chest. Alexandra moaned softly. In a panic she realised she was beginning to drown in a sea of treacherous longing, and worse, that in a few minutes she wouldn't even care.

'No!' she breathed as he pushed her gently on to the sofa.

'No?' he queried, as he bent to slant tasting kisses down her throat with lazy enjoyment. 'Do you expect me to believe that when you're starting to tremble?'

He'd always seemed to have the ability to note where each fastening was on whatever garment she was wearing before he pulled her into his arms. As she felt the zipper of her dress slide down, she pushed against him with a last reserve of determination.

'Jim, no,' she said, before confessing in a desperate panic, 'All right, I'm still attracted to you . . .'

'That's all I wanted to hear,' he said huskily as, combing his hands into her hair, he kissed her with a hungry passion.

The intense rocketing of pleasure made her realise his hand had found the softness of her breast. If she didn't stop him now, it was certain that she'd end up in his bed again. She broke the kiss and gasped, 'Jim, that's enough! Stop it, do you hear?'

'Just let go, Alex,' he breathed.

'*You* let go,' she insisted, trying to fight him off.

It would have been easier if her senses hadn't been so pleasure-drugged from the possessive way he was arching her to him. She thumped her fist against his shoulder, struggling so wildly to get free that she almost fell off the sofa. Jim caught hold of her to save her but, not realising it, she struggled with such desperate violence that she tumbled in an undignified heap on to the carpet. He went to help her up, but she scrambled to her feet, pulling her dress back over her shoulders.

'I should have known better than to have trusted you!' she raged as she hurried into the hall to pick up the phone.

She had her hand on the receiver when he covered hers forcefully with his own.

'What the hell are you up to now?' he demanded.

'I'm ringing for a taxi to take me home. I'm not staying here with you one minute longer. All you want is to get your hands on my baby, and you're prepared to use the most despicable means to get what you want!'

She shoved her elbow hard into his ribs, and with a growl of surprise he released his grip on her hand. Immediately she snatched up the receiver, only to have it pulled out of her grasp and banged down on to its cradle.

'Don't be so damned stupid!' Jim exploded. 'I'll take you home.'

'Not while they still run trains from Rickmansworth station you won't,' she snapped, making for the front door.

She just reached it before he slammed his hand against it, barring her exit. With concentrated fury he said, 'I've resisted the impulse to shake you on more than one occasion. In view of your condition, I'll resist it yet once more. But you'd just better get in the car this minute.'

His tone warned her to do as he said.

CHAPTER ELEVEN

THE ROADS were empty and Jim drove fast. Alexandra made no attempt to break the dense, taut silence between them. A glance at his taciturn profile told her he was still angry with her. His strong jaw was an uncompromising line, and in the glow of the dashboard the vertical lines of his cheeks were more noticeable.

But if he was angry, so was she. What alarmed her was that she was simmering with such emotional resentment that, if she allowed herself now to be drawn into another fiery exchange with him, she wasn't sure what she might end up saying. She hadn't ended their marriage with such fierce self-control to erupt into a series of bitter, tearful reproaches now. It was infinitely better to withdraw into herself, not to let him see how vulnerable she was, how much he had, and still could, hurt her.

He pulled up outside her house. She was about to say a very cool goodnight to him when he caught hold of her by the arm. His dark eyes held hers, a flicker of annoyance still in their depths, though it scarcely showed in his voice.

'Alex, listen,' he began. 'I've made a mess of this.' He glanced away and gave a brief, mirthless laugh. 'It's funny, in the business world I always get it right, but with women . . . Well, you've always been an enigma to me.'

'I resent that,' she told him, clinging determinedly to her chilly poise as her last defence against him. 'I am not irrational, impossible, volatile or any of the other things you've called me lately.'

She wasn't sure whether it was her remark or her delivery of it that amused him, but faint humour touched

172

his mouth as he said wryly, 'Let's just say I've known other women who are a lot easier to understand.'

She didn't doubt it, but as Jim evidently intended the remark to signal a truce she didn't come back with a sharp reply.

He saw her to the front door and then with a certain exasperation he said, 'I've gone about this all wrong. I ought to have whisked you away somewhere. You're too elusive—you always were. If I could get you alone on a desert island, I might begin to fathom you.'

'Desert islands are few and far between,' Alexandra said quietly as she found her key and opened the front door.

Jim put his hand on her arm, delaying her.

'When am I going to see you again?' he asked.

She disliked the purposefulness in his voice.

'I don't want to see you for quite a while,' she told him, not troubling to hide her hostility. 'I was prepared to play fair with you and you just took advantage of me. Well, having thought it over, I don't really think I owe you anything. You're trouble, Jim. I had my whole future sensibly mapped out till you reappeared on the scene and disrupted everything——'

'That's right,' he cut across her, his tone jeering. 'You were going to marry Roxby. Exactly why, I still haven't worked out, in view of the fact that you weren't in love with him.'

'I don't know what gave you that impression,' she retaliated with a defiant lift of her chin.

A few seconds ago the tension between them had been ebbing to a gentle poignancy. Now it was vibrating dangerously again, linking them together so that she could no more shut the door than he could turn away.

'Normally,' Jim said sarcastically, 'when a man and a woman are in love, they end up demonstrating their feelings for one another by going to bed together.'

Her eyes warred with his for an instant, and then she conceded with bad grace, 'All right—I wasn't in love with Roxby.'

'But you were quite prepared to marry him.'

'And why not? I was fond of him and we got on well.'

'You and I get on well and, furthermore, you're expecting our baby.'

He was tripping her up on her own arguments. But, however sharp his reasoning, he wasn't going to defeat her.

'Jim, we've been through this,' she said. 'I'm not going over it all again. We're not on a desert island, and however much I might regret it, life is not made up of wishes and dreams.'

He raked a hand savagely through his dark hair. He looked fed up beyond measure, and as though he wouldn't have minded hitting someone.

'You know something?' he said with curt anger. 'You're a fool. You're too idealistic to settle for a relationship that isn't showered all over with stardust. The only wonder is that Roxby ever got as far as he did with you. Someone should have told him that he'd stand more chance of taming a unicorn than trying to win your heart and soul.'

'You're right,' she flashed back, her voice suddenly catching, 'I won't settle for second best. I'd rather have nothing than a marriage that isn't based on love.'

'Then I'm sorry,' he said harshly. 'Sorry for us and sorry for you.'

He turned and strode off down the path. Alexandra watched him go, her throat painfully tight. But if she weakened and agreed to marry him she would only regret it. She simply couldn't take the risk of giving him a legal right to her baby in the event of a divorce.

North Wales was starting to seem like a haven. She was only sorry she wasn't planning a longer escape. Not that she was running away from Jim, because she wasn't. His final comment to her sounded as if he had finally accepted that he would never talk her into marrying him again.

She underestimated his tenacity. She picked up her post from the mat on Tuesday morning to see a white envelope addressed in his bold writing. Suspiciously she tore it open, not quite knowing what to expect.

He had sent her a card showing a moon-washed sea that created a shining path into a dark blue distance, and silhouetted in the foreground was a leaning palm tree. Inside the card he had written,

'We could always see if the desert island idea works. Isn't a spell alone together somewhere worth a try?'

She was on the point of tearing the card in two when she changed her mind. An offhand reply would spell out far more clearly that she was never again going to get involved with him. She added the words below his short message, 'Sorry, not interested,' found a fresh envelope and put the card back in the post.

Yet the card still troubled her faintly. She knew she was being over-cautious, but she decided it would be wiser not to give Ellen the address of the hotel she was staying at. Telling Ellen was almost the same thing as telling Jim, and she wasn't running any risks of him cornering her when her main aim in going to ground for a short spell was to recover from the emotional turmoil of the last few weeks.

But she was sure it was safe to tell her mother where she would be staying. She was still in the middle of packing when Olivia called round on Friday evening. Alexandra was pleased to see her and, not guessing there was any special purpose to her calling round, she chatted about her holiday preparations as she led the way upstairs.

'I'll just finish packing, and then I'll make some coffee,' she said as they went into her bedroom.

'Lovely,' smiled Olivia, sitting down on the bed.

Alexandra slipped a dress off its hanger and then glanced at her, querying her look of bright anticipation. Catching it, her mother laughed and said, 'Well, come on, pet, don't keep me in suspense any longer! Have you accepted Jim's proposal yet?'

'Mother,' Alexandra began, 'didn't you listen to a word I said when we went round Harrods together?'

'*Yes*,' Olivia protested. 'But I didn't think you really meant it. I mean, you told me you and Jim were having dinner together at the weekend. I've been expecting all week that you'd phone me.'

'There's nothing to tell. We discussed the baby and . . . Look, nothing has changed from when I spoke to you last.'

'But why?' Olivia wailed. 'You have a perfectly good offer of marriage from a man who's willing to keep both you and the baby. And you must love him at least a little, or you wouldn't have got pregnant in the first place.'

'Oh, Mother, can't you understand?' Alexandra sighed in sudden desperation. 'If I didn't love Jim so hopelessly, perhaps I could marry him. But he's only asked me because of the baby, and I can't bear to ever have him hurt me again . . .'

Her voice broke and she looked down at the dress she was folding, trying to hide the fact that her eyes were filling with tears. For an instant there was a stupefied silence, and then Olivia stood up. Hugging Alexandra briefly, she said throatily, 'I just didn't realise—you never said. But, darling, are you sure Jim . . .?'

'Yes, I'm sure,' Alexandra interrupted, fighting hard to keep her voice steady. 'Jim's only concern is the baby.'

There was a long pause, and then Olivia said, 'Well, you know I'll do everything I can to help.'

She had to smile at the note of purpose in her mother's

voice. Although Olivia was capricious, it was comforting to know she intended helping with the baby.

Alexandra got on the road early the next morning. She decided to make the drive part of the holiday by taking the A-roads and stopping off to wander round Worcester and Ludlow. From there she made for Welshpool, the rolling countryside of the Borders giving way gradually to a wilder, harsher scenery of austere grandeur.

The road running over the massive shoulders of the mountains was overtowered on her right by an almost sheer, scree-scarred ridge. To her left, a valley dropped away to a swiftly running stream where the grass was cropped short by the ranging sheep. Among the summits of the pass, with the afternoon sun turning everything to brilliance, her troubles seemed already to be receding.

She arrived at the hotel at just after six o'clock in the evening. Set high up off the road where it overlooked the estuary, it hadn't changed at all in the three years since she had last stayed there. Her room gave her a beautiful view through the hotel's steeply terraced gardens and the larches to the broadening estuary and the towering ranges beyond.

She spent the next few days visiting places of local interest and relaxing in the grounds. Having left her problems beyond the pass, she was thoroughly enjoying the holiday, even if she didn't have anyone to share it with. The hotel staff were friendly and she was lucky with the weather. It was warm and sunny, and she decided to take the receptionist's advice and spend an afternoon on the beach at Fairbourne.

It was too chilly to swim, but ideal for a walk barefoot along by the water's edge. Carrying her sandals, she strolled over the sand towards the sea. The breeze tugged at her hair and the gulls' piercing cries rose in sharp, keening volleys above the roar of the waves. The tide was out, leaving behind clear, sun-warmed pools to wade through.

She walked some way before heading back up the beach to perch on a bank of pebbles. Cupping her chin in her hands, she gazed out to where the sea broke white-crested, listening to its irresistible call.

Her thoughts settled on the baby and a womanly contentment enfolded her. Her career was satisfying and rewarding, but it couldn't touch the deeper fulfilment that the knowledge she was going to have a child gave her. She felt strong and at peace with herself.

Surprised, she realised she could look back and see the mistakes she had made. She had struggled hard to get where she had with her career, but although the break-up of her marriage had been partly her fault the rift that had developed between her and Jim hadn't been caused by her fight for success.

It had come about because, while she was perfectly eloquent and coherent in an unemotional legal argument, she'd never had the same fluency when it came to talking about her feelings. She'd always expected Jim to guess what she was thinking. When she had asked for a separation, it had been in the hope that he would force her into discussing what was wrong with their relationship. *She* should have been the one to insist that they talk. Perhaps if she'd communicated with him better from the start, he wouldn't have been unfaithful to her. Even with the baby, she knew she would always crave the challenge and stimulus of legal work, but never again would she use it as an escape from the intricate puzzle of human emotions.

She picked up a rounded pebble, feeling its dry smoothness between her fingers. It had taken all this time to understand herself. Yet if fate hadn't stepped in she might well have gone ahead and married Roxby. A crease of puzzlement appeared between her brows. Had it been fate, or had her subconscious had anything to do with this? She must have known deep down that her fiancé wasn't right for her. Never for one moment, if she'd been honest with herself, had she stopped loving Jim. Was it possible that, without knowing it, she had wanted to get pregnant by him? It was quite a thought. Getting to her feet, she shook the creases out of her skirt, fastened her sandals and headed back thoughtfully to where she had parked her car.

She drove back to the hotel. As she walked up the steep incline from the car park to the porticoed entrance, she debated whether to go straight to her room to wash the sand from her feet or into the bar for a long, cold drink. The cold drink won.

After the bright sunshine, the tiled foyer with its bursts of greenery seemed dim and cool. Pleasantly tired from the sun and sea air, Alexandra headed for the bar, not noticing immediately the man who was reading a newspaper in one of the deep armchairs. It was only as she approached that he leisurely folded the paper and said casually, 'Hello, Alex.'

She gaped at him.

'Jim!' she breathed accusingly, strength coming back into her voice as she exclaimed, 'I don't believe this! How on earth have you tracked me down? I deliberately didn't tell Ellen where I was staying.'

'No, but you told Olivia,' he supplied, getting to his feet.

He was in jeans and a casual shirt, and his dominating height and closeness seemed to positively threaten her. She couldn't retreat into formal remoteness with him now, not when she was wearing a button-through cotton skirt and thonged sandals, and her hair was loose and windblown. In any case, she was still reeling from her mother's connivance.

'I have to hand it to you,' she said short-temperedly. 'I never thought I'd have to put up with Mother conspiring with you. Well, let me know the worst. Where are you staying?'

'Here. Where else?'

'I thought so. In which case, I'm checking out.'

Jim caught hold of her elbow, redirecting her from her intended direction towards Reception and steering her towards the bar.

'I've just driven over two hundred miles to talk to you,' he said amiably.

'Do you really expect a thank-you for that?' she snapped with hostility. 'I came up here to get away from you!'

'It won't hurt you to have a drink with me,' he said.

Despite his easy-going tone, she had the intuitive comprehension that he would force her to make a scene before he allowed her to resist him. Reluctantly she agreed, 'OK—one drink.'

It would at least give her a few minutes to work out her strategy of defence with him. In keeping with her image of the self-possessed, independent woman, she stayed with him as he went up to the bar. The barman, who was about twenty and trained to be friendly without intrusiveness, nodded to her in acknowledgement.

'What will you have?' Jim asked her.

She felt as if she needed something bolstering to stiffen her defiance.

'I'll have a brandy,' she said, turning to the barman to give the order herself.

'Spirits are bad for the baby,' Jim told her. 'A Dubonnet with lemonade for my wife, and I'll have a half of bitter.'

The barman took the information about Alexandra with

scarcely more than an intrigued flicker. She waited till Jim
had handed her drink to her and she was sitting opposite
him at a table next to the window before she hissed, 'Do
you know, you really infuriate me! I'm booked in here as a
single woman, and you've just let drop that I'm pregnant!
This isn't London, and attitudes aren't as broad minded as
at home. Added to which, I'm not your wife any more.'

'That's what I'm here to correct.'

He leaned back in his seat and ran an idle hand down his
glass before letting his gaze meet hers. He seemed so
relaxed that she didn't sense that it masked an underlying
tension. She gave a short exasperated sigh and said 'I'll say
one thing for you—you don't give up.'

'You're right, I don't,' he agreed firmly. 'Not when I
think I'm in with a chance.'

'Hell will freeze over before I marry you,' she told him
with crisp clarity.

'Is that because you're afraid you can't make a
relationship with a man that works?'

She was too startled for an instant to reply. Then she
managed derisively, 'Where did you get that amazing idea
from?'

'Ellen. I went to see her. I thought she'd be able to tell
me where you were, but she couldn't, so I tried Olivia. She
was even more interesting. She says you're in love with
me.'

Alexandra leapt to her feet in one furious movement,
betraying colour rushing to her face. Her heart was racing.
The citadel had finally fallen to Jim's attack, and she
couldn't even begin to refute his statement, let alone be
laughingly contemptuous. So that was what Olivia had
meant when she'd said she'd help in any way she could!

'I take your point,' said Jim with quiet forcefulness as,
taking hold of her elbow, he guided her out from the table.
'We'll finish this conversation somewhere quieter.'

They were halfway up the wide red-carpeted staircase before she had recovered enough to say, 'I can't begin to fathom why Mother should tell you anything so utterly ridiculous.'

'Neither can I, unless it's the truth,' he said, steel behind the lightness.

He escorted her down the corridor and, still keeping his hand on her arm, he unlocked the door to his room. Alexandra was about to protest when he marshalled her inside.

The room was well-proportioned, restful and full of sunlight. Two french windows opened on to a balcony which overlooked the glimmering expanse of the estuary. The beige brocade curtains were looped back in generous folds, and the same material covered the large double bed. By the window were two armchairs.

Pulling away from Jim, Alexandra advanced into the room, gaining a safe distance from him before saying stormily, 'You've wasted your trip, Jim.'

He came towards her and gripped hold of her shoulders.

'Alex, cut the pretence,' he ordered. 'You love me. I started to wonder if it was possible when I got to thinking about the remark you made about wishes and dreams. Now I've heard it from Olivia. I'm stark mad crazy about you, so why can't I hear it from you?'

His eyes held hers, the intense ardent light in them meaning that for an instant she almost believed his forceful words. Then sanity took over and she said tiredly, 'It's the baby you're crazy about, not me.'

'What the hell else did I have to try to persuade you to marry me?' he demanded, giving her a little shake for emphasis. 'I didn't know then that you loved me. The only argument I thought you'd listen to was one that was intensely rational.'

She stared back at him. Then, freeing herself, she said,

scepticism masking the hurt in her voice, 'And Juliette? I suppose she never meant anything to you?'

'I was never engaged to Juliette. I let you think I was to try to make you jealous. Ellen had obviously told you I was getting married. You jumped to the conclusion that it was to Juliette, and I didn't correct you.'

'Is that why you told her I was pregnant?' she asked. 'Or did you happen to mention it to all your employees?'

'I told Juliette you were pregnant because she'd asked if there wasn't some chance that you and I would get back together again. It's what she wanted. Believe it or not, she's always liked you.'

'How thoroughly altruistic of her!' Alexandra exclaimed.

'For pity's sake, Alex,' snapped Jim with exasperation, 'Juliette was never my fiancée. She's already married.'

'She's . . . she's *what*?'

'She's married,' he repeated, 'and has been for the last two years, to the man she used to live with. They've settled in Hull, but she'd been helping me out temporarily down here while my secretary's on maternity leave. And before you ask the next question, Juliette did *not* come to Switzerland with me. I said that because I was so damn mad at you that day.'

He saw hesitation flicker in her eyes and demanded, 'What do I have to do to make you believe me? I love you, Alex. I've done nothing but scheme to get you back from the moment I discovered you'd got engaged.'

'You schemed to get me back?' Alexandra faltered.

'Why do you think I tracked you down in Sorrento? I meant to try to rekindle things between us, only I lost my temper with you instead, and because of it checked out the next day. I couldn't believe my luck when you turned up on Capri.'

'But you said you hoped I'd be happy with Roxby,' she

whispered, her heart beginning to race.

'How far would I have got with you if I'd told you the truth? I'd walk through fire for you if I thought it would do any good. I've spent three years missing you. When I went to see Roxby with the intention of telling him he'd damn well better marry you, I knew if he refused I was going to ask you myself. I reckoned that once the baby was born I'd forget it wasn't mine. That's how much I wanted you.'

She struggled to find her voice, taking a halting step towards him, but all she could manage was a strangled, 'Jim . . .'

It was enough. Jim swept her into his arms, enfolding her so tightly to him that she could scarcely breathe. He muttered her name raggedly, and she wound her arms tightly about his neck, choked with happiness, until suddenly she again remembered Juliette. Her shoulders sagged and the elation faded. Sensing it, Jim stiffened, and as she put a protesting hand against his chest he let her draw away, a frown of puzzlement between his shrewd eyes.

'Alex, what is it?' he demanded.

She took a couple of harassed paces away from him before turning back to face him. On the beach this afternoon she'd made a resolution. She wasn't going to put up barriers any more, or suppress her feelings. Her voice was low and, although emotional, quite adamant.

'I believe you when you say you love me but, Jim, it's no good. I'm not going to marry you.'

A nerve twitched along his jaw, but he made no attempt to come near her. He stood there rigid with the effort of not crowding her.

'Why not?' he asked curtly.

'Because I can't take being married to a man who can't be faithful to me.'

In the nerve-tensing silence he again succeeded in keeping the channels of communication open between them by not exploding into forceful anger.

'What makes you think I won't be faithful to you? I've been faithful to you for five years. Since the day I met you I've either been making love to you or I've been celibate.'

The ring of sincerity in his voice made her heart tighten with a mixture of fury and pain. If he could be so plausible over this, she'd never be able to trust him.

'Don't lie to me, Jim,' she said with all the vehemence of anguish.

'I'm not lying,' he said, grinding out the words so that they were very spaced and very distinct.

'So you never had an affair with Juliette while we were married?' she said with bitter sarcasm.

'Juliette?' he repeated, as though he couldn't believe what he was hearing.

'Yes,' she replied, her voice rising angrily. 'Your wonderfully obliging secretary?'

'You think I had an affair with Juliette?' he demanded. 'Are you mad?'

'You see how hopeless it is?' she groaned, going to push past him and out of the room.

His former stoic calm meant she wasn't prepared for his next action. Swift as a hunter, he snatched hold of her and almost threw her into an armchair. She gave a faint, startled cry as she landed against the cushions. Putting his hands on either side of her on the arm-rests, he leaned over her, keeping her prisoner as he said, 'Now, you'd better say where you got this idea from that I ever had an affair with Juliette.'

'I saw you together,' she said, glaring at him. 'I came back home unexpectedly and she was with you. So don't lie to me, because *I know*. It was that weekend just before I told you I wanted a divorce. I came home . . .' Her voice caught before she managed to finish bitterly '. . . and there you were, the two of you, having a really good party together.'

Comprehension suddenly came into Jim's face, but not one trace of guilt. His eyes, dark and utterly serious, still burned into hers. In a low, driving voice he began, 'I remember that night. Now I don't know what you saw, or what you thought you saw, but I'll tell you what happened. You'd just told me you wanted a separation and then you'd gone off on the revision course. When the doorbell went I answered it with the crazy hope that you'd changed your mind, that you'd come back because you wanted to talk. Instead, Juliette was outside. A taxi had dropped her off and she was smashed, so smashed she could hardly stand up straight.

'I said I'd ring her boyfriend, and that started her crying. She sobbed out that it was all over between the two of them and that he'd walked out on her. During the row he'd apparently said she was no good in bed.

'You were threatening to leave me; I was at my wits' end to know what to do to keep our marriage alive. All I wanted was to sober Juliette up enough to take her home and then leave her to sleep it off. I was in the kitchen making coffee when I heard the stereo come on full blast. I went back into the lounge to tell her to turn it down, to find that she'd taken off all her clothes and was trying to play seductress with me. Shortly after that show-stopping performance she passed out on the sofa. It must have been after midnight before I got her home and thought it was safe to leave her.'

He stopped, and Alexandra stared at him, her eyes wide and shocked. She believed him, and yet it was almost too much to comprehend.

'Is . . . is that why she said those things to me in the restaurant that evening?' she murmured in a daze.

'Because you'd been kind to her and she though I'd walked out on you for no reason?'

Bending down by her chair, Jim seized hold of her hand.

'There was never anything between me and Juliette. She could have offered herself to me absolutely sober and I wouldn't have wanted to know.'

'Oh, Jim,' Alexandra said huskily, 'I'm sorry. I . . . I've been such a fool!'

Relief and gladness came into his face before he pressed her palm to his lips with such a depth of passionate tenderness she felt tears come into her eyes. Sliding her fingers lovingly through his hair, she whispered, 'Darling, why did you let me go? All you had to do was to ask me to stay and I would have done.'

He looked puzzled and said, 'You told me you wanted a divorce. Have you forgotten?'

'Only because I thought you were having an affair. I never wanted to end our marriage, but you seemed so . . . so indifferent.'

'Indifferent?' he repeated with a ragged laugh as he got to his feet. 'You'd got me defeated on every front. I'd known from the first that you weren't in love with me . . .'

'But I was,' she interrupted protestingly. 'I told you . . .'

'That you didn't marry me to get through law school? Alex, your whole life was structured around your career. You slaved over that course. Even when the sex between us was at its best, you started crying after I'd made love to you because I was demanding more from you than you wanted to give.'

'It wasn't because . . .' she interrupted as she stood up and went towards him. A sudden wave of understanding was clarifying everything. 'Jim, I . . . I only turned you down when you first asked me to marry you because I was afraid of loving you, of getting involved. And when I started to cry it was because . . . because I'd never felt the way you made me feel. Every time we made love it got more and more powerful . . .'

She broke off. She'd never talked like this about her sexual feelings before, and expressing herself was like a venture into foreign territory. She knew she was blushing, but she went on, 'When . . . when we made love you made me respond not just with my body, but with my mind, my whole being. I still want to cry when you make love to me.'

'Sweetheart,' Jim muttered raggedly, drawing her into his arms, 'why the hell didn't you tell me?'

'I just assumed you knew,' she whispered.

He gazed down at her, their eyes holding for a long moment before he cupped her neck with his palm and kissed her. She closed her eyes, a shiver of excitement going through her with all that his kiss seemed to promise her. His lips were sensuous and infinitely gentle, kindling in her a deep hunger for more.

When finally he raised his head, she traced her fingers caressingly along his jaw.

'I know I pushed myself hard over those exams,' she whispered. 'I was so frightened of failing—and maybe, too, I wanted you to be proud of me.'

'As if I could be anything else!'

He kissed her again with a deep yearning that sent hot flames of wanting dancing along her nerves. She could sense his need of her, but with everything certain between them there was no need to hurry, and taking things slowly with words and kisses and caresses could only heighten the ultimate pleasure of unity with each other.

Breaking the kiss, she ran her hands sensuously over his back, her eyes alight as she asked, 'Did you really intend all the time to get me back?'

Jim pushed her down on to the bed.

'I only let you go because I thought that if I didn't,

you'd start to hate me for depriving you of your freedom. But when Ellen told me about Roxby I was furious. I'd let you go to give you some space, not to lose you to anyone else.'

'And you said you'd no intention of ruining my plans!' she accused with a soft laugh.

'I'll admit, from day one I was out to seduce you,' he said with his attractive smile. 'The only thing I didn't plan was getting you pregnant. It never occurred to me that you wouldn't be sleeping with Roxby. I took it for granted you were protected.'

'No, *you* didn't plan it,' said Alexandra with a half-smile.

Humour and speculative curiosity came into his shrewd dark eyes.

'What are you saying, Alex?'

'You didn't know I wasn't protected, but *I* knew, and I know the likely outcome when two people make love. I certainly didn't think it consciously, but today when I was walking along the beach I just wondered if subconsciously I wanted to get pregnant by you.'

He murmured her name, kissing her again, his hands slipping beneath her blouse to stroke her skin. Excitement began to burn in her like a fever. When at last his lips left hers she unbuttoned his shirt, pressing small kisses against his skin. She felt a shudder go through him before he pressed her back against the pillows.

'Before we start to make up for three lost years,' he said huskily, 'there's just one more thing. I came here to put a ring on your finger.'

He stood up and fetched his jacket, taking out of the pocket a small jeweller's box.

'But I've still got the engagement ring you bought me,' she protested.

'You can wear it on your other hand,' he said, taking

the sapphire and diamond ring and slipping it on to her engagement finger. 'The ruby belonged to last time. Now we're making a new start, but with one major difference. Last time I let you go. But never again am I going to let you get very much further than an arm's reach away from me. Understand me, Alex. This time, it's forever.'

Delight was dancing in her heart like the diamonds in the ring. Her eyes full of answering love gave him the promise he wanted. Jim growled his satisfaction and leaned into her embrace as with a low, enticing laugh she teased, 'I love it when you're masterful!'

Amusement tempered for an instant the dark passion in his eyes. Then his embrace tightened and with a shiver of excitement Alexandra abandoned herself to his ardent, tempestuous lovemaking.

They were going to laugh together and she was going to love him till her last breath. She would share the depth of herself with him in countless conversations, in the thrilling and varied joy of their lovemaking and through their relationship with their child. Finally she had come home, and home was sharing her life with him.

VOWS   *LaVyrle Spencer*   £2.99

When high-spirited Emily meets her father's new business rival,
Tom, sparks fly, and create a blend of pride and passion in this
compelling and memorable novel.

LOTUS MOON   *Janice Kaiser*   £2.99

This novel vividly captures the futility of the Vietnam War and the
legacy it left. Haunting memories of the beautiful Lotus Moon fuel
Buck Michael's dangerous obsession, which only Amanda Parr can
help overcome.

SECOND TIME LUCKY   *Eleanor Woods*   £2.75

Danielle has been married twice. Now, as a young, beautiful widow,
can she back-track to the first husband whose life she left in ruins
with her eternal quest for entertainment and the high life?

**These three new titles will be out in bookshops from
September 1989.**

W●RLDWIDE

*Available from Boots, Martins, John Menzies, W.H. Smith, Woolworths
and other paperback stockists.*

4 ROMANCES & 2 GIFTS - YOURS

ABSOLUTELY FREE!

An irresistible invitation from Mills & Boon! Please accept our offer of 4 free books, a pair of decorative glass oyster dishes and a special MYSTERY GIFT...Then, if you choose, go on to enjoy 6 more exciting Romances every month for just £1.35 each postage and packing free.

Send the coupon below at once to -
Reader Service, FREEPOST, P.O. Box 236, Croydon, Surrey CR9 9EL

✂ - - - - - - - - - - - - - - - - - - - *No stamp required* - - - - - - - - - - - - - - - - - - -

YES! Please rush me my **4 Free Romances and 2 FREE Gifts** ! Please also reserve me a Reader Service Subscription. so I can look forward to receiving 6 Brand New Romances each month, for just £8.10 total. Post and packing is **free**, and there's a free monthly Mills & Boon Newsletter. If I choose not to subscribe I shall write to you within 10 days - I understand I can keep the books and gifts whatever I decide. I can cancel or suspend my subscription at any time, I am over18.

EP60R

NAME ———————————————————————————

ADDRESS —————————————————————————

————————————————————————————————

———————————————— POSTCODE ———————————

SIGNATURE ————————————————————————